FIRE ON THE LIPS

FATHER SPYRIDON BAILEY

Also by Father Spyridon

Journey To Mount Athos
The Ancient Path
Trampling Down Death By Death

FIRE ON THE LIPS

ENCOUNTERS WITH A SAINT

FATHER SPYRIDON BAILEY

FaR

Published in 2015 by FeedARead.com Publishing.

Financed by The Arts Council of Great Britain

Copyright©FatherSpyridonBailey

The author or authors assert their moral right under the Copyright, Designs and Patents Act, 1988, to be identified as the author or authors of this work.

All Rights reserved. No part of this publication may be reproduced, copied, stored in a retrieval system, or transmitted, in any form or by any means, without the prior written consent of the copyright holder, nor be otherwise circulated in any form of binding or cover other than that in which it is published and without a similar condition being imposed on the subsequent purchaser.

A CIP catalogue record for this title is available from the British Library.

To Joseph
for your encouragement and keen eye.

1975

Making the lecture took a lot of effort. I was in another seminar on the far side of campus and had to break into a run to make the start time. As I jogged past other students who barely gave me a glance I could feel my temperature rising and I began to worry that I would arrive only to sit sweating for an hour which was the last thing I wanted. The only reason I was going at all was to impress a girl I had met and being doused in perspiration was not going to create the impression I was hoping for.

I made the hall with a minute to spare but Julie was not around to witness my prompt arrival. This annoyed me a little: I felt my efforts deserved at least a little acknowledgement. The art department was a section of the university I rarely visited as my studies were devoted to the more serious matters of philosophy and English, and the display of paintings around the walls gave an impression of bohemia which left me feeling a little straight laced. I was dressed in the usual mid-seventies hair and denim, but really a big part of me was still the lad keen to do well and please his parents.

She appeared from a door at the back of the hall and just as it had done every time I had seen it, her face struck me as something more than beautiful. There wasn't a piece of art inside any of the frames around us that was more carefully crafted. I was punching above my weight and knew full well that life would never offer me anything better. There are plenty of pretty faces in life, but I convinced myself that this was more than simple attraction; on seeing her for the first time it had been as though she was instantly familiar. I managed to subdue an emerging grin before it pulled my face into an unflattering pose.

She was followed by a tall man dressed in a dark robe, his dense beard too black to belong to English skin. As much as I was hoping to catch Julie's attention my focus now shifted as I found myself staring at this strange figure. There was something I couldn't explain about him, a feeling that was unknown to me. He looked to be in his late twenties but it was hard to be sure as he had the air of a man much older. He glanced around the group of students before him and smiled gently before taking the seat offered to him by another young woman from the art department.

The two women chatted quietly for a moment, obviously agreeing last minute details, before Julie took a seat near the bearded man while her colleague stiffened as she prepared to address us. The audience was made up of about thirty students and a few lecturers; I had found a seat at the very edge of the group. Julie at last caught sight of me and gave a little wave: I was surprised to realise how much this little gesture meant to me but above all I was relieved my efforts had been noticed. I smiled and returned the wave, satisfied that sitting through the next hour was now worth the effort.

"Thank you all for coming," the other woman's nervous delivery made us feel a little uncomfortable, "it really is a great honour to be able to welcome Father Basil to come and speak to us." She turned to acknowledge him and he gave a small nod of the head in response. "This lecture is part of our history of art module, can I remind all of you on the course that there will be a seminar following today's lecture in Mr Thomas' office on Thursday." She glanced down at a sheet of paper to satisfy herself that she had included everything that she was meant to mention and then waving her hand towards him announced "Father Basil."

He got to his feet and stood silently for a moment as though gathering his thoughts. That brief moment was stretched out in the sense of anticipation felt by everyone watching him. I glanced across at Julie who looked as transfixed as everyone else as she stared at the back of his head. We had a better view of him now and I was struck by the angles of his features. There wasn't an ounce of fat on him, his cheeks were sunken and only the thickness of his beard gave an impression of width to his face. There was a severity to his features, it was a face carved by a lifestyle I didn't understand, but this sobriety was softened by his eyes. They looked out with a genuine compassion that seemed unhurried and full of peace. It was a presence that was comfortable to be near and any resentment I had felt at having to give up my free time now vanished.

"Thank you," he spoke with the hint of an East European accent which he would later identify as Romanian. "I have been invited to talk to you about icons and the development of their use in Orthodox spirituality. As you can see I have only a single sheet of paper for notes because I feel that if I plan what I am going to say too strictly it will prevent me from hearing the Holy Spirit. To speak on such matters we must be open to the words God would have us speak, our good intentions too often get in the way of this. This is true when we are giving lectures, like today, but of course in ordinary life too when we think we are addressing the person before us, but really we are working through our pre-planned script of things we want people to think about us. This prevents us from seeing and hearing the other person and we are often left only with the image we have chosen to create for ourselves. This is really a form of idolatry since we can do the same thing with God, even worshipping our own ideas of Him rather than seeing the truth He reveals of Himself. So let us try to be open now and we can perhaps all learn something today of what God wants us to know. I have heard very little in life from carefully planned scripts that is worth remembering, but often people will speak spontaneously and the mystery of God is touched. So when I have finished you must ask me lots of questions, and perhaps we can all learn something."

These words struck me immediately; I could sense the truth of what he was saying as though they were coming from some inner voice from deep within me. He continued with a brief explanation of how icons had found their place in the life of the early Church. Much of what he said might as well have been in Romanian for all the sense it made to me, ancient history was not a subject I concerned myself with. But through out his talk there were other comments that struck me again and again like arrows. Though only vaguely affected by my Protestant upbringing I would have identified myself as Christian if anyone had been bothered to ask. But nothing I had heard from our local vicar carried the weight and authority of the things that seemed to pour so effortlessly from this man. His words touched a reality that I had never been aware of. He made reference to a world of experience that was completely absent from my own imagined journey. Calling my self a Christian was clearly very different to anything he was referring to. Although I had no desire to become a card-carrying member of any denomination I did want to hear more.

He picked up a large icon that had been lying on the table beside him. I knew enough to recognise Saint Mary holding Christ as a child, but it was an image I had never really looked at in any detail. If pressed I might even have been able to describe it from memory, but now I began to look into the image in a new way as Father Basil spoke. He paused for a moment to allow us to connect his words with what we were seeing and I began to sense something of how the artist had captured the mother's tenderness for her son. Her head was tilted towards Him in a posture that communicated the very human relationship between them. It was something I had never before considered, that Christ would feel towards His mother the way any of us would respond to a loving parent. The artist had captured this in a deeply moving way but had avoided being sentimental. There was the same sober reality in the painting that I had recognised in Father Basil's face.

Catching myself in this moment of contemplation a shudder of anxiety passed through me as I remembered my father's warnings about worshipping idols. An unpleasant sense of contradiction filled me as I struggled to connect the devout man before us and the image he was holding which I was struggling to accept as anything other than an object of idolatry. I shifted uneasily in my chair, I just couldn't resolve the tension I was feeling between knowing that this monk was obviously a committed and intelligent man and his apparent willingness to contravene such a central commandment from God.

The hour passed quickly, and he repeated his invitation for questions. I wanted to demand an explanation to my concerns but didn't want to risk upsetting Julie. One or two people managed to demonstrate their knowledge with some clever questions and Father Basil patiently gave his answers. When it was clear that no more questions were coming Julie's friend stood once again to address us.

"Thank you so much for that Father Basil; it has been an incredible talk." It was clear to everyone that she meant it, and a few people nodded their heads in agreement. "You've really brought this subject alive for us and I know it's going to be a great help to those of us working in this area for our assignments." She paused and looked at one of the lecturers, then added "Thank you once again." She invited applause and it was given with some enthusiasm to which Father Basil responded by looking at the ground before him as though he was unaware it was meant for him.

Chairs scraped on the hard floor as everyone got to their feet and began to talk. My original plan had been to dash to Julie's side and congratulate her on organising the event but without any thought or hesitation I made straight for our speaker. At the time I couldn't have accounted for my actions, but I strode over to him before anyone could engage his attention.

As I approached he looked up from the icon he was wrapping, the same warmth still shining in his eyes.

"Father Basil," I blurted, "may I ask you a question?"

He stood to his full height and I found myself looking up at someone well over six feet tall. His presence as a speaker had been full of humility and

I hadn't realised what a large physical presence he had. "Of course, how can I help you?"

"Please forgive me, but doesn't it say in the Bible that we are not to create graven images or worship anything other than God? How can you use icons in the way you have described knowing this?" The question sounded much more abrupt than I had intended but I was glad the words were out.

"Yes, it is true that we must avoid worshipping idols, but your question shows a misunderstanding of how icons are used." He spoke calmly and I was relieved that he hadn't taken offence.

"When you worship God, do you do so just in your mind or do you think God wants the whole of your being to be active?"

"All of me," I said.

"Then should not all five of your senses be involved in what you do in worship? Your ears hear the melodies, you smell the candle wax and incense, your body moves and adopts postures – you kneel, you stand, and so also your sense of sight should be included in worship too. When you fill your eyes with beauty that is offered to God doesn't this help you to draw closer to the giver of all beauty?"

Despite agreeing with his point I wasn't satisfied, "Yes, but creating beauty is one thing, why must it be an image of Christ?"

"It is not always Christ portrayed in icons, as you have heard today many icons carry images of the saints. But the icon is simply an image of those who are near, the saints are with us in our worship, along with the angels, and God is present everywhere. The icon gives a visual sense of the reality that we believe and touch through faith."

He paused to allow me to absorb his words, all the time his brown eyes shining.

"I accept what you say, but icons are physical objects, God is spirit. How can you use them this way?"

"The Church teaches that Christ's incarnation changed the whole of the created order. Just as He sanctified the water by being baptised, so He has made the sanctification of all creation possible by entering and living within it as a man. The very things of the earth, wood, paint, eggs and so on, can now be used in worship since God has transformed the very nature of existence."

"I accept that," I continued to resist, "but the Bible says you must not worship anything but Him. Are you worshipping icons?"

"Let me use an idea to help you. Have you ever received a letter from someone you love who is far away?"

I nodded my response.

"Have you ever found yourself holding that letter to your chest or even kissing it?" He could see in my face that I had. "Is your kiss for the paper and ink, or is it meant for the one who sent the letter, the one who is represented to you by the letter?"

I felt awkward even answering, but admitted "The person."

"So it is with the icon. We do not worship the icon as we do God, that would indeed be idolatrous. But when we kiss the icon we kiss the image of the one for whom the honour is given. The icon is like a window to the heavenly reality through which in faith we are able to look to see this greater reality. Through the physical object the mind is taken beyond the physical present to the spiritual reality beyond."

"I understand that," I persisted, "but why do you have to venerate them? Isn't it enough to just look at them and use them to help you think about these things? I can't get to that point beyond the looking."

"Do you not venerate the symbol of the cross? Why should you not also venerate the image of God? To do so is to proclaim that He has truly taken our flesh; He is not unseen any longer. We venerate the image of the face that is truly Christ's. You exist as both body and soul, and your spiritual nature needs the physical in order to both experience and express your life. So too we receive the spiritual reality through the physical one, we are not denying or cutting off the physical world as Christians, but drawing it up into our worship of the One Who created it. We pray to those portrayed in the icons through the icons. Our prayer reaches beyond the surface of wood and paint. Every icon of Christ is a proclamation that God truly did become a human being Who could be seen, touched and yes, even painted."

I was unprepared for any of this and knew I wanted to understand more but I didn't have the questions necessary to find what I wanted. I was overwhelmed and needed to think about what he had said. At that moment Julie appeared at my side looking a little concerned at what she was hearing of our conversation.

"Is everything alright?" She enquired.

"Yes, of course," I managed to say quickly in order to prevent Father Basil the opportunity to complain about my response to his lecture. She offered her hand to him

"Thank you for helping us out, it has been a pleasure hearing what you had to say."

He shook her hand but then turned back to me once more. "Here is my card, my telephone number is on there, please contact me at the monastery if you would like to talk further or just come and see what we get up to."

I took the card, thanked him, and stepped back to allow Julie to usher him away. By now most of the audience had wandered off except for a couple of small groups deep in conversation amongst the otherwise empty rows of chairs. I watched Julie lead Father Basil back through the door from which they had first emerged and then realised I hadn't made plans with her about whether I should wait for her to return. I took a seat on the first row and lent across the back of the chair beside me. The conversation had affected me but I wasn't focussed on any one thing he had said. It was the impression of the man himself that I was feeling, and I was unsure how to categorise him. Further questions now began popping into my head and I was frustrated with myself for not having thought of them earlier. He had communicated a peace that had somehow found its way inside me, it was a feeling I wanted more of.

I looked up at a large clock on the wall and wondered how long I should wait. I was prepared to sit for as long as she would take if I knew she was definitely coming, but the uncertainty sapped my patience. I gave it a long ten minutes more and then gave up. As I was heading out I heard Julie's voice calling me and the fuss of feelings I'd been carrying to the lecture resurfaced. I turned to find a satisfied smile on her face and I instantly knew I wasn't in trouble.

"Well done, that was great," I offered.

"He was an excellent speaker, and a really nice man. Mr. Thomas made a point of telling us what a good job we'd done organising it."

I leaned close and kissed her, hoping it would come over as some kind of congratulatory gesture, but to me it was just an opportunity to kiss her. She slipped her arms around me and returned the intimacy; the closeness of her body was a magical gift from the universe. We were twenty-one years old and would never know this careless happiness again.

1976

Eight months into our relationship we had settled into a comfortable state where the chase was long forgotten but the excitement had not yet dwindled. We could bicker without fear of revealing something hidden and the world around us had come to accept us as a couple. We were in our final year of university and wondering where the next stage of life was going to take us. It was a feeling of limitless possibilities but also the realisation was dawning that we would have to make a decision about how committed we were to each other: there was also the reality of geography to think about as we came from different ends of the country. Romance is easy when it demands no sacrifice, but the easy days and easy choices of student life were coming to an end.

My studies were gong well and on the face of it I had nothing to complain about. But the reality was there were questions gnawing away at me that I couldn't answer. The transition to early manhood can be tricky for a lot of us, but my issues were metaphysical rather than emotional. I looked at the world around me and I knew I was getting a pretty good deal compared with many people. I wasn't struggling to put bread on the table or fighting a corrupt government for basic freedoms. I wanted for very little and yet there was an emptiness inside me that I couldn't put a name to. I knew there was something missing and I began to wonder if it was a spiritual issue. Although I had a vague belief in God it wasn't a faith that did much to me: it was really nothing more than ideas and notions.

I hadn't given Father Basil much thought since his lecture but coming across his card in my jacket pocket one day I stopped short and found myself reading and rereading the telephone number of the monastery. Without mentioning it to Julie or anyone else I made my way to the telephone box at the end of the street where I was living and began dialling the number. I didn't have any exact notion of where it might lead, but I felt an impulse to speak to him.

I heard the telephone ringing at the other end and after a few seconds someone picked it up. I dropped the two pence coin into the slot and nervously enquired after Father Basil. I gave my name and explained "He told me to ring on this number."

"I am sorry but the fathers are unavailable at this time of day, please ring back before lunch tomorrow."

I was disappointed at the news but thanked him and hung up. I wondered if this was meant to be a sign that I shouldn't pursue my quest but then rejected the idea as silly. I trudged back through the rain trying to imagine what the monks would be doing at that moment and conjured up a suitably holy scene to satisfy myself that I was doing the right thing. As I walked some of the things Father Basil had said at our meeting began to return to me and for a brief moment I remembered the peace his presence had communicated. It was enough to encourage me on and I resolved to make the call the following day.

I was sharing a meal of rice and unrecognisable vegetables with Julie that evening when I casually mentioned my intention to ring the monastery again.

"I tried to ring Father Basil today."

"Really!" She was genuinely surprised, "why?"

"Don't worry, I'm not feeling the call to become a monk. I just had a few things I wanted to talk about."

"Is everything okay?" She frowned, "are you alright?"

"Yea, fine, I just wanted to..." I couldn't explain it. "You know, just talk to someone about a few things. I found his card and it seemed like a good idea."

"Are you sure there's nothing wrong?"

"Honestly Julie, don't worry. There are a few ideas I've been wondering about, that's all."

"Why do you need to speak to a monk about them? It seems a bit extreme."

"What do you mean extreme? It's not extreme at all. I was remembering some of the things he said at your lecture, I thought it would be interesting to talk to him again. Don't blow it into anything more than it is, I don't know why you're responding like this."

"I'm not responding like anything, I just don't understand why you've got to go running off to see a monk. It seems a perfectly reasonable thing to ask."

"You were just as impressed with him as me; I remember how you went on about him."

"Yea, from a history of art perspective," her frown got deeper, "not as a guru giving life advice."

"Think what you like, I'm gonna ask if I can visit in the holidays. Don't make an issue of it, I thought you'd be interested."

We finished our food with little conversation. Afterwards she disappeared into the kitchen to wash the pots and with a perfunctory kiss announced that she was going back to her place. I was a little hurt but also relieved to not have to explain myself any further. My reluctance was not any aversion to sharing what I was feeling, but really a product of my confusion. Julie's response had only made me see more clearly that I couldn't explain my motives either to her or to myself. It wasn't a comfortable realisation and I didn't like the sensation of not understanding my own impulses this way. I pushed the thoughts from my mind and found a book I was reading. It filled my head with distractions and the questions no longer needed answering.

The following morning I was in the telephone box again with more coins than I would possibly need; I was determined not to let even the tiniest of glitches get in the way.

"Hello, I rang yesterday, my name is Stewart Lee, is it possible to speak to Father Basil?"

"Yes, wait one moment; he is in the studio."

I could hear footsteps approaching on a hard wooden floor and then Father Basil's familiar voice answered. "Hello?"

"Father Basil, my name's Stewart, I met you at Cardiff University last year, you gave me your card after the lecture."

"Yes, I remember you, how can I help you?"

His question felt too direct and I wasn't sure I could give an adequate answer. "I'm not sure, I was wondering if it would be possible to come to speak to you some time."

There was a pause which filled me with anxiety, but then he came back on the line, "Yes, of course, I have my diary open, when would you like to visit?"

It was another four weeks before I made it to the monastery. The journey took most of a day, with three train transfers and as many different buses. I was exhausted as I walked the last half mile from the last bus stop following the directions Father Basil had dictated to me over the telephone. I had been invited to stay for two nights which would give me a single full day around the monks. I hoped to see exotic towers or domed roofs as I approached and was a little disappointed to discover a group of rather humble looking buildings. The complex was a development of an old farm house and a few out-buildings but the large three-barred cross over the gateway at least conveyed a small sense of what I was hoping for.

There was no sign of activity and I found myself immediately affected by the stillness of the place. To the back of the monastery rose a gentle hill and out in every other direction the views were of fields and woodlands. The absence of activity did not feel like emptiness, and though at the time I dismissed it as nothing but my imagination, I was aware of how the silence felt as though it was filled with an expectation that extended beyond my own human longings.

I nervously approached the front door of the main building and stood listening for a moment hoping to catch the sound of someone inside. My furtive actions were rewarded with only more silence and so I knocked firmly against the wood. The sound felt intrusive but I was relieved to hear the same sound of footsteps I had heard on the telephone. The door swung open before me and I was greeted with the familiar face of Father Basil which broadened into a wide smile at the sight of me. He stepped out and greeted me with a strong embrace as he kissed my cheeks. I found my face buried in a beard that was much longer than it had been the year before and which was filled with the scent of incense.

"Welcome to the monastery Stewart, how are you?"

"I'm good, thank you Father."

He led me inside and after enquiring about my journey disappeared into the kitchen to make coffee. I was left in a room that had low benches along each wall, it was clear that good sized groups could be accommodated here quite comfortably. I sat at the table near the only window and tried to gather my thoughts before his return. I calmed my breathing and struggled to form a reason for why I had come. My mind went blank, there was no single point I could make and I knew I wouldn't be able to explain myself.

He returned with a tray and laid it before me.

"The other monks are helping a local farmer cut down some trees on land not far from here. They will be back in time for prayers."

He fixed his gaze on me, and without speaking I could sense him drawing me forward to express what was in my heart. "I don't know how to explain why I'm here Father, I just had a sense that I should come."

He nodded, and as he began pouring the coffee said "How are things at university?"

"Good thanks, we're nearly at the end of the course, and then we start looking for jobs."

"What kind of work do you see yourself doing?"

"I'm not sure, it sounds ridiculous, but I still haven't found anything that I want to spend the rest of my life doing."

"It is important to take your time; you must ask God to guide you in this choice. The work we do in life can have an enormous effect on our spiritual well-being. We can become very frustrated or depressed if we take the wrong job. You must reflect on your skills and seek to find a way that God would use you. We are all given different abilities which form the One Body, real peace can be found when we are obedient and use what God gives us for His service. So often I meet people who have ignored their natural talents or worse tried to use them for their own ends rather than in God's service. For example, think of a man who is blessed with great speaking skills, who can inspire people to achieve what they might otherwise think beyond them. Such a man could use these skills to encourage people to great acts of charity or service of others, or else he might convince people to buy used cars or invest their money in him. People might look to the former and say that God has given him these skills, but the truth is those same skills can be turned to selfish aims. God grants us the freedom to use our gifts as we will, but there will be a time when we must account for what God has loaned us." He paused in thought for a moment and continued "What may be a great skill can easily become a source of evil. This principle is true within each of us; our strengths can so often become mirrored by failings. Someone who is very sensitive to the people around him can easily fall into man pleasing, or someone who is decisive can easily become insensitive to the wishes of others. To identify where we need to repent we often need look no further than what we consider are our strengths."

"I find myself wondering about even more basic things than this Father, sometimes I am not even sure what I am."

"What do you mean by this Stewart?"

"I don't know what it really means to be a human being, I find myself unsure about how I'm different to my parents' dog. I know I have rational thought, but is that it? Is the only real difference between us and animals the capacity to think rationally and be aware of ourselves thinking? It doesn't seem enough of an answer. I probably sound ridiculous to you saying these things"

"You don't, but to answer your question, it doesn't seem enough because it isn't enough of an answer." He smiled for a moment, "you must recognise the true worth of yourself as a human being."

"I'm not sure where to begin," I admitted, "all I have is...," I searched for the word, "confusion."

"You are not alone in this; it is a good start that you are able to see your confusion. Most people in the West have not yet recognised how far their ideas of themselves have drifted from reality. All of us suffer delusion about ourselves, of course with respect to our sinfulness, but also in terms of what we are."

"Forgive me Father, but what are we then?"

"When we look at the creation of the world we see how God made all things. With a word He commanded that there be light, and without anything more light came into existence. Light which gives us sight, which is so filled with colour, which symbolises so much, was created with a simple command. So it was with all things, the stars, the seas, the animals and trees, everything except us." As he paused I could see the brown in his eyes glinting with clarity and focus, the soft humility that had first drawn me to him was now mixed with a sharp certainty as though his words were being pulled from the deepest part of himself.

"God did not create man in this way," he continued, "it was not a simple command from God into the universe that brought us into being like the creatures already made. The Holy Trinity spoke within Himself, He said "let us make man", He pondered over our being. The Divine Creator of all things pondered over us, and then made us in His image and likeness. We are given a dignity that extends beyond all else in creation because we bear God's image." He smiled at this thought and I could sense how deeply he understood the meaning of what he had said, but I was still uncertain.

"I have heard this description Father, but I don't understand what that means. I realise it doesn't mean God looks like us, that it isn't our physical form that reflects God's image, but which part of us does?"

"You are right, it is a delusion to imagine that God can be reduced to a body like ours, and many opposed to Christ have often accused the Church of believing such things. When Scriptures speak of God's hand, or God's eye, or God doing something in physical terms, it is metaphorical language used because the truth of God is a mystery beyond our knowing. Always remember that God is incomprehensible to the rational mind, He cannot be contained or limited. The human body is corruptible and so cannot contain within it that which is incorruptible. The human body grows old, grows weak, gets sick and dies: how could such a thing be created in the image of God? The human body is weaker than that of many animals. A man cannot pull a cart like a horse, he cannot fly across great continents like the birds in migration, if he falls into the ocean he will be overcome by the strength and speed of a shark. And yet, though he is physically weaker than many creatures he subdues and dominates the earth. So then, we must look elsewhere, to the inner nature of man to find the image of God."

"Do you mean his rational powers?" I asked. "Isn't it simply man's rational capacity that allows him to dominate other animals?"

"Yes, certainly, our rational powers are an important part of the inner man. The soul is given the capacity to choose, to reflect, but it is more than the capacity to solve mathematical puzzles or build bridges. The rational man must dominate, but not just the outer world. Within the soul is the capacity to rule over the passions, to determine the appearance of the soul itself."

"Do you mean by following the commandments, by choosing to avoid sin?"

"You are partly right," he smiled again, "but the authority and image of God is not given to man carved in stone tablets, it is written in the soul itself. The words are not commandments carved to be read, they speak within us as a voice to which we can be obedient or which we can ignore."

"Would that be what we often call the conscience?" I asked, still unsure.

"The conscience is a part of what I am talking about, but the image of God is much more than this of course. We are created in God's image and with this comes a responsibility to rule over physical nature and also our inner nature. Cultivating the fields or breeding livestock is merely an outward pastime, but we are commanded to take sovereignty over our soul: and yet we, who are created to rule more often become slaves to the passions. We demean ourselves when we give up the responsibility to rule, we give away our dignity by submitting to the power of pleasure and bodily desires. This is how the rational mind may be used to reflect the image of God in ourselves, when it is in control over the inner life of man, electing to dress the soul in obedience and virtue and shun that which God warns is harmful."

He could sense that I was struggling to process everything he had said. He gave me a moment in case I wanted to ask another question, then stood and carried the tray back into the kitchen. I didn't think to offer to wash up; I was filled with the reality of his words which had opened up to me beyond their surface meaning. I could sense something about my own existence which was beyond anything I could have imagined before having this conversation. It was as though he had simply pointed to something for me to look at and having seen it I was now able to observe it at will whereas before I had been unaware even of its presence. It came with the realisation that I had not lived up to the responsibility he had talked about and that rarely had I made any effort to take control of my inner self. It occurred to me that for much of my life I had been stumbling blindly through my days pursuing the various goals that promised happiness or achievement or what I imagined to be security. But it was all dominated by the demands of the outer world and of my material existence. Even the flimsy moral framework I liked to think I had been following was really one more expression of my own wishes and constructed by circumstances and upbringing.

To recognise so much of my self as meaningless was frightening, it was like suddenly waking from a twenty year dream and seeing my self for the first time: and not seeing anything of worth.

Father Basil returned and invited me to take a walk with him. "It will do us good to get some fresh air. I will show you our gardens."

The ground was dry as we headed down across the field in front of the house towards what looked like a small shed. As we walked I began to express some of my feelings.

"Father, I am still unsure how to think of the difference between myself and other creatures. I think I understand what you are saying about taking control of the inner self, but is this the only difference between us and the animal kingdom? I see so many similarities when I think about how animals live and behave, it confuses my thinking."

"Yes there are many similarities, but even within these we can recognise the worth of man that is so much more than other animals. For example God created the different creatures to multiply and fill the earth and to man he appears to give a similar commandment to multiply and grow. Like the other creatures we come into being in a form that must grow and mature, but God's commandment to us extends beyond this. Though our physical form will reach its limit of growth after twenty-one years, the inner man must continue to grow in virtue: the image of God within us must continue to overcome our sinful passions. The process of our purification is an eternal growth that no other creature has been blessed to share in. Similarly the command to fill the earth means not just physical reproduction but to fill creation with the glory of God. When we live out the commands of God we share His love and His Kingdom grows. We are made co-workers with God, He has entrusted us with this work. But this reminds us also that the image and likeness of God are two things. We are first created in the image of God, but must grow in His likeness. We must use the authority God has given us to become like God."

I looked at him with concern at these words; it felt as though he had gone beyond what he meant to say. "Do you mean that literally?"

He gave me a patient smile, "Yes, this is our ultimate purpose. So often you hear people in the West wondering about the purpose of life as though it were some mysterious quest. And in some ways it is a great mystery, but in others it is a simple and obvious thing. God is different to us in His nature because He will always be the Creator and we will always be His creature. There can be no confusion about this distinction, for God alone is to be worshipped. But this is the dignity and worth of man. That we are made to grow in His likeness so that we share in His divinity. not by nature, but by grace. God chooses to lift us to such heights but gives us the responsibility of choosing to participate. What kind of divinity can there be that is not freely chosen or does not exert itself to reject evil? Our calling is to grow in God's likeness so that we may become perfect, even as our heavenly Father is perfect as our Lord commanded us."

I had never heard such things before; it was as though Christianity itself had been half hidden from me, portrayed as one thing to conceal another. My whole life I had been told that a Christian must try to live a good life in the hope of achieving a heavenly reward. The morals and teachings of the faith had been reduced to a set of rules that must be sufficiently followed in order to win the game. Hearing Father Basil's words at once made sense to me and I recognised the emergence of a greater picture that I was beginning to see a small part of.

It sounded a ridiculous thing to say once the words were out, but I had to ask, "Does this apply to women too?"

"Of course, it is the inner person which grows in this likeness, not the outer physical form. In fact I have met many women whose patience and love exceeds anything I have witnessed in a man. Though their physical form is more delicate, the souls of women are often more refined than that of men. It is through this love and the patient endurance of evil that we become like God, through goodness and communion. I have spoken of how we dominate other animals, and in our masculinity we have overcome even bears and lions from which all other creatures on earth will run. But the inner beasts are harder to overcome, the passions that enslave us. Again, I have met many women who exhibit great control over these beasts, and many men who are dominated by anger or lust for power or greed. Do not imagine that the outer form of a person is any indication of the inner reality."

I felt suitably admonished but was still glad I had asked the question. As he spoke I had begun to think of Julie and as far from perfection as I knew she was, I also knew that she had greater control over her passions than I could ever hope to achieve.

As we approached what I had thought was a shed I saw that the monks had built a sheltered place for prayer out in the field. It resembled a small, open-ended bus stop where it was possible to pray before a large icon of the Theotokos that had been hung there. Father Basil crossed himself and then knelt down in the grass.

"Let's say a prayer together," he invited.

Rather self-consciously I knelt beside him, and found myself looking into the face of the same icon he had brought to the lecture at the university.

"We can say the Lord's Prayer," he said, "do you know how to intone it?"

"Do you mean sing it? Not really."

"That's alright, we'll just sing it on a single note." He bowed his head and then began to intone the familiar words I had repeated so often as a small child at school. There was a beautiful tone to his voice, even as he sang on a single note, and once I had begun to sing along the self-consciousness left me. Words I had spoken with what amounted to no more than a kind of muscle memory now seemed to express more than the words themselves, it was as though they carried my inner self to God. As we finished the prayer he crossed himself again and we rose to our feet.

"There you see another way that our humanity has been dignified by God." He continued to look ahead at the icon as he spoke. "God has become one of us through His mother. The Maker of all things lowered Himself to enter the womb of one of His creatures in order to raise us up to be like Him."

As I looked at the painting the relationship between mother and child took on a different meaning and I saw in her tenderness for her son the trust which God had shown to humanity. The Son of God had been nurtured and protected by ordinary human parents in all their frailty and poverty. The risk that this entailed was vast, and yet God knew the heart of Mary whose obedience became the link between Heaven and earth.

"Christ's humanity was not an illusion," Father Basil explained, "while remaining God He became man. Our humanity was then taken into God as Christ ascended. Christ's humanity is an eternal part of Him; it has not been cast off. The union of man and God in Christ is the likeness to which we climb. She was not only the mother of Christ, but the mother of God. Christ was truly God on earth, and she remains His mother for all eternity. Do you see now something of the dignity that God has granted us? How much higher is the place of man than that of the common cattle or birds or fish?"

I nodded my understanding; I was seeing both my self and him in the light of his words and felt changed by their impact. We continued to walk down to the bottom of the field where we came to a number of canes and glass-topped boxes. Everything was neatly laid out in rows and conveyed a sense of order and many hours of work. He began to point out the different vegetables that were growing and broke off some sweet peas for me to taste. Though they were not quite ripe they were still delicious.

"Most of our food is grown here at the monastery, but through our icon painting we are able to pay for additional supplies." He began to walk on past the gardens and I assumed I should follow. By now the monastery buildings were out of sight and other than the fences that divided the fields there was no obvious sign of human life. Early evening was beginning to colour the sky and the world around us felt alive and good. The things Father Basil was saying left me with the sense of us both belonging to and being different from the created order around us. I was filled with a sense of peace and gratitude simply for being there at that moment, it was as though I knew there was nowhere else in the world that could feel more right or have anything more to offer. It was more than contentment, it was a feeling that there was no past chasing me or future pulling me forwards, only that present moment where everything was as it should be.

We walked along one of the fences and then at the corner of the field turned back towards the monastery. He could see that I was out of breath as we climbed the incline and he waited for me to recover. I felt a little awkward at having to be given this time to rest and tried to cover this with more questions.

"Where do our thoughts fit into what you have been saying? There are moments when I have random ideas that pop into my head, they trouble me at times."

"This is common to all men; you must not allow them to rob you of your peace. Do not engage with them, recognise them as not belonging to you and simply allow them to drift away. There have been holy monks troubled with such things for long periods of their lives, but it is not anything to be concerned about so long as we do not allow them to stir up our emotions."

"I sometimes worry that I have no control over my thoughts when it happens," I added.

"Just as we must become master over the passions it is necessary that we rule also over our thoughts. When inappropriate thoughts come to us we must not pursue them or allow them to grow into fantasies. There is an ancient teaching that warns that we will not be judged by God for not having ruled over lions, but we will be judged for not having ruled over our minds and hearts. Thoughts that prompt us to anger, or lust or any of the passions are destructive and we must reject them when they come. This is what it means to rule over our minds, not that we can always prevent such thoughts suggesting themselves to us, but that we do not join ourselves to them. It is good to have to engage with such struggle, without them we could not learn to exercise our will or develop discipline. If our minds were permanently free of these thoughts who amongst us could be judged as worthy of reward? But since we must actively overcome them God sees our willingness to struggle for the sake of His kingdom and rewards us."

He could see my breathing was back to normal and again we set off up towards the buildings. The air was turning cooler now that the sun had had fallen below the hills and it was soon going to be dark. As I reflected on his words Father Basil seemed to sense the questions I was beginning to ask myself.

"When God made man He did so not just by a command but by using the dust of the earth. Again we are reminded in this both of man's lowliness and of his worth. The whole cosmos was created by a simple command, but when God created man He moulded him as an artist, putting himself into his work. It was even man's body which God took such care with, we see that this material existence is not a worthless garment but a precious gift in which God has placed us. But we see too that God took such care with the substance of the earth, a low and base thing. So man's value is not to be found in the physical substance of his being, but in the shaping that God took such care over. And into this form God breathed life. God shared, in some mysterious way, the life of Himself, in His own image and likeness, and we are called to live in a way that reflects this dignity. Our words, thoughts and actions should aspire to the high rank of God's image, and we must treat each person we meet as a living example of this truth."

Only now could I begin to see why Father Basil had such patience and kindness, his actions conveyed the worth he recognised in other people. Knowing how far short I had fallen in living up to this reality I felt ashamed to know how highly he considered me as a human being, it was like being a beggar wrongly crowned at a coronation.

Outside the front door he said "It's nearly time for prayers. I have to prepare the church, would you like to come with me?" I was keen to see it and followed him to the smaller building at the back of monastery. From the outside it looked unimpressive, it was clearly well cared for but other than a wooden cross over the doorway there was nothing that would distinguish it from any number of buildings on farms up and down the country. Once inside however, I discovered a room of colour and beauty. The walls were filled with life-sized frescoes of different saints which gave an impression of being surrounded by their presence. The iconostasis was adorned with icons obviously painted by the same hand as the frescoes and around the icons vines and fruit were intricately carved into the wood.

Father Basil began his routine of crossing himself and bowing before each of the icons. After each set of bows he reverently kissed the hands or feet in the image and moved to the next. While he was doing this the door opened and a second monk entered. He politely acknowledged me with a nod of his head and proceeded to venerate the icons in the same way as Father Basil. I watched as they then started to light the lamps hanging beside the icons. As the natural light was fading these glowing points of light shimmered as they were reflected in the gold of the paintings. The room quickly took on a magical atmosphere; I felt the sense of timelessness of what I was witnessing, practices that had been repeated for over a thousand years.

The two monks took their places at a stand to one side of the chapel, and by candlelight found the right pages in various service books resting before them. Father Basil indicated with a wave of his hand that I should move beside them and as I approached they began to chant. Their voices blended in the way only those who have spent many hours singing together can achieve. Despite the tones of their voices being different, together they seemed to join into a single voice of prayer. They began to take it in turns to intone various prayers in Greek, and though I couldn't understand the specific words, I felt myself drawn into the worship. Some of the psalms were printed in

English and Father Basil pointed at lines, encouraging me to join in. It was a kind gesture but I wasn't comfortable doing it, I felt too much of a tourist to be so involved, and I was relieved when they went back to their Greek.

The thin, brown beeswax candles gradually burned down to stumps as the service found its way through the various books that the monks kept opening. It was a complicated service that I would have had difficulty following even in my own tongue, but instead I found the rhythms of their voices carrying me forwards. There was no expression of emotion in their voices or actions, only the constant offering of prayer that structured their lives.

As they closed the books and began to blow out some of the candles I realised it was over and without thinking made the sign of the cross over myself. As an Anglican it was not something I was used to doing but it felt natural in this context. Without a word Father Basil ushered me out of the chapel and we returned to the main building.

"Please take a seat, Father John will be with you in a moment." I sat at the table and listened to Father Basil as he began preparing food. The outside world seemed a distant reality; all its pressures and worries had faded from my mind. Father John entered and smiled, he looked to be in his early forties, his beard was long and flecked with grey. He took off his hat and sat across from me before asking where I had come from and how I had heard of the monastery. I summed up the events that had led me there and still felt that I couldn't give a proper account of what had brought me to them.

As he listened he stroked his beard thoughtfully as though I was sharing the most important news he had ever heard.

"You must not worry about explaining why you came to be here, God plants holy desires within us to help us on our journey. Just be thankful and take what you can from the experiences he gives you."

We chatted a little about the monastery grounds and Father John explained the short history of their community. There had been monks here for twenty-five years, he had been there for fifteen of them and Father Basil had arrived nine years after him. He mentioned a third monk, Father Luke, who had left to visit another monastery, and in the way Father John described him it was clear that he held him in great respect.

Father Basil emerged with steaming pans and the two monks laid out the plates and cutlery. We then turned towards some icons on a low shelf behind me and they sang prayers and blessed the food. The meal was simple but hot and filling and I was grateful for it. They ate in silence and at a speed that surprised me. Julie was always complaining about how I bolted my food and it amused me to imagine how she would react to this scene. After the food they sang further prayers and refused my offer to wash the dishes. Father Basil made tea and poured us each a cup.

"Stewart and I have been talking about the value of man Father, about the image and likeness of God."

"Yes, a good topic," said Father John, "it is something I so often see missing in the modern world. Mankind has become so proud of its achievements, many of which are truly astounding, like putting men on the moon, but what is any of this compared with the image of God in each of us. When European thinkers became so convinced of the infinite possibilities of the human mind they discarded the true potential which is to become gods. Scientists dissect nature into tiny parts but they are so busy looking through their microscopes they miss the big picture. Science is a wonderful blessing, it reveals to us so much of what God has done. But we are so desperate to pat ourselves on the back we do not see what nature has to truly reveal. Look at the moon. It is so perfectly sized and so perfectly positioned that when a lunar eclipse occurs man can discover secrets of the universe otherwise completely hidden. Scientists take this knowledge and expand their theories, but ignore the simple reality that the moon is three hundred times smaller but three hundred times closer than the sun. Such an accident they say, but nature is full of these so-called accidents. Is it an accident that the only place in the solar system where such scientific observations are possible just happens to be the one place where intelligent creatures exist to make these observations?" He glanced at Father Basil and my self; he seemed uncertain whether to continue. We nodded our encouragement to which he continued "But in the confusion of theories man has lost his vision of who he is. Darwin tried to lower us to nothing but one more beast amongst many, and in truth many men live as though they were just beasts. But we must hold tight to the precious reality of who we are if we are to live as God wants us to. I tell you, there is not one scientific discovery, not one machine or invention that has a fraction of worth of any one human being. All the achievements of man fall into insignificance compared with any one human soul. And so many people live in ignorance of this. They become depressed; they doubt the purpose of their existence, because they do not know how precious they are to God." By now he was warming to his subject and the words poured from his mouth in a torrent of enthusiasm. "But when they are liberated from the *isms* of modern thinking they find the ancient reality which has been hidden from them."

Abruptly Father John stopped and looked a little sheepish, "Forgive me, I have said too much."

"No Father," I assured him, "I am grateful for your words."

"Father John worked as a physicist before entering the monastic life," Father Basil explained, "he has written a number of books on this subject –

some of which are much too clever for my understanding." He laughed a little and it seemed to relieve Father John of his discomfort.

"I wrote those books too soon, someone should have told me to sit silently in my cell for a few decades before even considering putting pen to paper. When I look back I see much of what I wrote is unnecessary. But pride will make us do many foolish things." He smiled to himself and his presence had softened again.

After the tea Father Basil led me a guest room next to the church. He invited me to join them for prayers at 3-30a.m. if I wished, or for the Liturgy which began at 7a.m.. I opted for the later time and thanked him for everything. The guest room walls were clean and bare, there was a single bed beneath a window and a small table beside it on which sat a jug of water and a drinking glass. Above the bed hung a small printed icon of Christ, His face had been made to look stern but also with an expression of understanding. I got changed and lay in the dark for a while, running through some of the things Father Basil had said. The monastery felt like a secret place which the world knew nothing about. That such lives were still being led in the twentieth century seemed remarkable, and as I contemplated such things I happily drifted off to sleep.

The alarm clock pierced the darkness and for a moment the strange room left me disorientated. Once I had my bearings I was glad to be facing a new day here and I quickly dressed and prepared my self for the service. It was still dark when I reached the chapel which was illuminated by the globes of light around the candle flames. A new voice was leading prayers, a priest I hadn't met before was standing at the altar leading the service. Father John was now dressed in his deacon's vestments and Father Basil stood at the choir stand as he had the previous evening. My entrance went unacknowledged and I found a discreet place to stand. The Liturgy moved forward with its own momentum, the prayers and responses following each other in a natural pattern that maintained a steady rhythm. Father John began censing the icons and the clouds of sweet smelling smoke curled and climbed through the church, adding to the sense of mystery and beauty.

The priest emerged from behind the iconostasis with the chalice and with great reverence Father Basil was given communion. After receiving he moved back to his place, head bowed low, he now seemed almost oblivious to anything around him as his focus turned entirely inwards to his meeting with God. His outward appearance was still, but it was clear that within him something limitless and beyond words was taking place. I caught myself staring at him as he became transformed; his appearance was drawing me to him, and in the end out of politeness forced myself to look away.

By the time the Liturgy was ending rays of morning sunshine were streaming in from the windows through the drifting incense. I began to wish that Julie could have been there to witness it, it would make sense of everything in a way that any explanation I could give her never could. The priest appeared once more, this time holding a basket. Father Basil motioned for me to approach and I was given a piece of blessed bread. It was dry and difficult to chew but I didn't care, I was pleased to be able to participate in some way.

After the Liturgy we gathered around the now familiar dinner table while Father Basil prepared breakfast. The visiting priest was from a parish located about an hour's drive away and he explained how he came once a month to serve the Liturgy with the Fathers. He was a small, grey haired man who had a very serious demeanour, he spoke very little and I didn't once see him smile. He and Father John discussed some of his parish business as I sat quietly waiting for Father Basil's return.

Breakfast consisted of fruit, bread and pasta; I was becoming used to the idea that the humble food of monks could taste better than the rich meats of the world. After we had eaten Father Basil cleared the table and Father John and the priest had business to attend to in the icon studio. Father Basil returned to the table with a fresh pot of tea and I was glad to have him to myself once more.

"We were discussing the nature of human beings," he said, "I felt we were getting somewhere."

"Yes Father, your words helped me a lot. But I'm struggling with other things."

"Please, feel free to raise anything you want."

"What you said about human dignity makes sense to me, but I can't reconcile this with how sinful I am." I felt relieved to have admitted what I was feeling.

"Is your question about a particular sin you have committed, or are you thinking more widely about man in general?"

"Yes, I suppose I am thinking about evil in general. I'm not sure how to think about it."

"It is a very big topic Stewart, but let us begin with the basics." He paused as though he were wondering where to start. "God created all things good, and to man he gave free will. So we must first understand that nothing evil was created by God. But if the choice to love is real, so must the choice not to love. Love cannot be forced on any one; if we were compelled to love then it would not really be love. But the reality of our not choosing love is evil. We each give ourselves to evil when we fail to love. So we can see that the consequence of our rejection of love is suffering."

"Yes Father, this makes sense to me, but what about the devil? Where does he come into all of this?"

Father Basil nodded at my question, "Satan was an angel who through pride rejected the worship of God and wanted to make himself the object of veneration. How often does pride make each of us guilty of such folly? Whenever we imagine ourselves worthy of any kind of praise we fall into the same sin as Satan. Since what is evil cannot remain close to what is pure, Satan was cast out from God's presence and with him a third of the angelic hosts which we call demons. The reality of spiritual warfare is too often ignored by western Christians, and yet, whether we know it or not, we each live on the spiritual battlefield. Our thoughts and actions participate in that warfare, we must struggle to become aware of all that we do as having spiritual significance."

"I have heard this before, but I still can't connect it with our experience of evil. Why would the devil want to harm us if he is really angry with God?"

"Satan has become so corrupted and blind by his own evil that he is unable to see how to repent or find God's salvation. But seeing all that God does to save mankind he turns his anger against us. Since Satan cannot fight against God directly, he turns his hatred and anger on those who are created in God's image. Satan recognises what we are, he sees the image of God within us more than we do ourselves. He fabricates all kinds of illusions and lies to lead us astray, and when we blind ourselves to God's truth we easily fall prey to Satan's deceptions. The mind is easily led astray, it is important to guard ourselves against any fantasies or images that come to mind in prayer. Even if an angel of light were to appear to us the Church Fathers warn us not to receive it. We must remain simple and humble, do not expect or desire so-called spiritual experiences; longing for such phenomena only lead to destruction. The reality of God's presence is enough; we do not need to see lights or angels."

I sensed that Father Basil was not merely recounting teachings he had heard from others, it was clear from the way he spoke that this truth was something he lived personally and of which he had had direct experience. I asked "How do the demons attack us Father?"

"There are many ways that the demons wage war on us. You must remember that they have lived through many centuries; they have gained great experience in plotting the downfall of man. They are devious and clever and we must avoid allowing them a foothold in our lives. This is why we should seek simplicity, because we cannot outwit them at their own corrupt games. Their attacks on us may be outer or inner, through things or through thoughts. We see, hear and feel the outer world, and often these are enough to lead us astray without any demonic involvement: we are capable of enough greed and lust that the demons' work is done for them. But thoughts are another thing. It is easy enough for us to fast, keep vigil and avoid the traps that the body may fall into. A reasonable amount of ascetic practice will help us in our struggle with outward things. But our thoughts can only be controlled when we achieve a purity within the soul: this is a much greater and difficult task.

Just as control of how much food or sleep we permit the body helps to avoid being enslaved by it, so the soul must be treated with its own means of purification. The soul is purified by forgiveness, mercy, love of God and neighbour. The soul requires far greater treatment than the body, but both must be purified if we are to be restored to the likeness of God."

We had come full circle and I realised that Father Basil was still explaining to me something of the subject he had begun the day before. Though I had felt like I was raising new topics for discussion he was carefully guiding me to see the one bigger picture he had begun to previously unveil. There was a twinkle in his eye as he saw my realisation and the smile returned to his lips.

"Yes," he said, "it is all part of the same truth."

The monks' day was structured in a way that having slept through the night I was out of sync with them. They took some hours of rest in the morning while I set off to explore some of the countryside and reflect a little on what I had been hearing. I somehow managed to lose my way and a good part of the day had passed by the time I found myself climbing the hill back towards the monastery again. Ideas about the human body were still running through my mind and I couldn't help but feel something of a contradiction in my understanding. It didn't make sense to me that something created by God could become the means of the soul's destruction and I was determined to put this question to Father Basil. The opportunity didn't come until after evening prayers when I found myself sitting at the usual place at the table.

"Father, may I ask you to explain something to me? I am a little confused."

"Of course, what is it?"

"How can the body be such a source of temptation if it is created with such purpose by God?"

"First you must remember that all of creation is not as it should be. Not just our bodies but the trees, the birds, the planets, the whole cosmos exists in a fallen state. When Adam chose his own will over the law of God the consequences were truly cosmic. Satan sinned in the heavens, but Adam sinned in Paradise. And so the earth now exists in anticipation of redemption which comes moment by moment as human beings choose obedience and love. Each time we repent and seek to serve God we participate in this cosmic restoration, this is the high calling God has given us."

I nodded, "Yes, but how can the body be different things simultaneously? Am I to hate it or give thanks for it?"

"It depends. Part of the spiritual process is to learn discernment, it is crucial and few people have this gift. This is why we monks seek the guidance of an elder who has this gift, because otherwise we are allowing chaos to determine our path. But as for the body, discernment permits us to know when to treat the body as an enemy, but also when to treat it as a friend or even comfort it as a invalid. It is important to distinguish which is right because if we alienate the friend or welcome the enemy it can quickly turn against us. In Orthodoxy we speak of the royal way, which is to avoid extremes. There is a saying that anything to extreme is of the devil. So over-indulgence is obviously harmful, but so is fasting to the point that we make ourselves sick. Enough care must be taken over the body that we keep ourselves healthy and able to work and pray, but laziness and gluttony is an invitation to many other passions. Does that make sense to you?"

"It does, but what you say about our fallen state, does that mean that just as the soul is purified so too the body can be redeemed?"

"There are two parts to your question." He paused for a moment, wondering which answer to give first. "The answer is yes, the body is redeemed. At the day of resurrection we will all be raised in bodies that will not corrupt. It will be a universal event for all people, and the body of each will be restored to its pre-fallen state. But your question implies something else, about the body in the time between then and now."

"Yes," I said, "can the body be redeemed before the resurrection?"

"The process of perfection is not completed in this life, otherwise there would be saints many centuries in age who had not died. But we see the signs of redemption in many saints' bodies. The union of soul and body is such that as the soul draws closer to perfection it becomes so grace-filled that it cannot but affect the body. This is why when some saints die their bodies do not corrupt."

"I'm not sure what you mean," I frowned as I spoke, "how do their bodies not corrupt?"

"When the graves of some saints are opened their bodies are found not to have decomposed. Saint Spyridon's body is nearly two thousand years old and yet it has not corrupted. Saint John of Shangai was buried in the cathedral in San Francisco and his body was also found to be this way. It is natural if you think about the link between body and soul, and is one of the blessings God gives to the Church to help us remain faithful because we are weak."

"I had no idea about this," I admitted, "forgive me, but it sounds too incredible to be true."

"I have seen Saint Spyridon with my own eyes, and on his feast day a sweet scent is emitted from his body. This is common knowledge in the Orthodox world." He smiled at my surprise, like a parent seeing their child discover something new in the universe. "There are many things you will learn to be true which at first do not fit into the world view you have been taught, but you must ask yourself who taught you to see the world this way? Most of our schools promote atheism and a narrow materialistic understanding of the cosmos depriving children of the wonder of its truth. Is it any surprise that we grow up complaining that we can't hear

God speak when we have put so much effort into closing up our ears?"

Our conversation turned to more mundane things and he described to me the organisation of the Church around the world. It was interesting enough but my heart was desperate to be fed more of things we had been discussing earlier. I was tempted to try and return to the topic by prompting him with a question but the opportunity didn't present itself. Father John joined us for final prayers and eventually we made our way back to the chapel. In the short time I had been there the monks had spent many hours in prayer and I understood that the things Father Basil was sharing with me were really just the tip of a huge and mysterious ice berg. I could see that real understanding did not come through conversation but through a life dedicated to God. However, this did not prevent me from feeling grateful for what I had learned from them. As the prayers drew to a close I began to think about my return to the world and all that it would entail. I prayed for Julie and for our future together, and I wondered how much of all this I would be able to adequately describe to her.

To my disappointment Father Basil had to leave the monastery as he was travelling to Ireland to make arrangements for an icon the Roman Catholic cathedral in Dublin was commissioning. Before he left he kissed my cheeks and hugged me once more, "You must come again soon Stewart, it has been a great privilege for us to have you here."

These words caught me off-guard and I didn't know how to react. Without any fuss he turned and was gone.

I chatted a little with father John who was keen to tell me about his work before he became a monk. He was generous with his time and made me feel very welcome, but I was happy to finally get to bed and bring the day to an end. I lay in the clean white bedding still contemplating the ideas that Father Basil had shared. Anglicanism had brought me to the door of something bigger, but I could see that in order to step through it I would have to face some difficult decisions. The combination of fresh air and lots of exercise had left me ready for rest and I had no trouble getting to sleep.

The following morning I over-slept. I hadn't set my alarm properly and by the time I was up Father John had eaten. I didn't mind missing breakfast but I was embarrassed to have risen so late. He neither laughed it off nor treated it as a problem; he simply wished me a good morning as though it were perfectly normal to lie in at the monastery.

"Father, thank you for letting me stay, I am very grateful to you all for the time here."

"You are very welcome Stewart, would you like a coffee before you go?"

"No, thank you, I must make the station or I'll miss my train. Please pass on my thanks to Father Basil."

"Wait, there is something I can give you." He opened a cupboard drawer and pulled out a knotted black rope. "Take this prayer rope with our blessing." It was small enough to fit comfortably around my wrist; I slipped it on and thanked him for it.

He accompanied me to the door and wished me a safe journey. I thanked him once again and set off up the track which had brought me here two nights before. As I re-entered the world I began to think about bus timetables, train connections, college assignment dead-lines and Julie. The peace of the monastery was something I could remember, but even as I was sitting on the first bus of my journey my head was already becoming crowded with a million unnecessary thoughts.

1977

The next ten months were full of change. Julie and I graduated and found ourselves jobs, and the new sense of ourselves focussed our minds on where our relationship was heading. Marriage seemed the next logical step and we happily made our plans for the future. I maintained my link with Father Basil through the occasional letter, and though I often thought about him I couldn't find a reasonable excuse to visit again. Julie viewed each envelope that came from him with a certain amount of suspicion but since I wasn't talking about him she seemed content not to make an issue of it. With work came a little bit more money, we bought a car, and generally began to feel that we were finding our feet. We were still young enough to be living quite carelessly, but our relationship was old enough to give us some security.

Julie had been raised a Baptist, her parents were fairly evangelical; they looked at my Anglicanism as being a little too liberal for their liking. Not that we were living out the teachings of any particular denomination, our Christianity was pretty neutral in its colour, we made it to church a few times a year, and generally thought of ourselves as moral people. This to us seemed the limits of its demands, or at least the limits of what we were inclined to do.

Looking for clean socks one day I found, pushed to the back of the drawer, the prayer rope that

Father John had given me. Its abandonment made me uncomfortable, I sensed a missed opportunity but couldn't have explained it any more than that. I held it up and examined it for a moment then slipped it on to my wrist as I continued searching for matching socks. Only later as I sat at my desk did I notice it again, it reminded me of the long versions wrapped around the monks' wrists and how they were constantly running the knots through their fingers.

I slipped it off and began running it through my fingers. The physical sensation brought back the smell of incense from the monastery church and I was filled with a sudden urge to return. I pushed it back on to my wrist and pulled down the cuff of my shirt to conceal it; such thoughts could only lead to trouble. I gave it no further thought and returned to the papers on my desk and the world of work quickly numbed me to anything more.

Later at dinner I was opening a bottle of wine and Julie caught a glimpse of the rope.

"What's that you're wearing?"

I instinctively moved my hand to hold it, "Oh, it's just a prayer rope that one of the monks gave me at the monastery last year."

"Why are you wearing it to work? It looks a bit hippy."

I laughed, "I don't know, I came across it this morning and put it on without thinking." I was trying to downplay its significance.

"What's it for?"

"For each of the knots they say a prayer. It's just a way of counting off without having to think about the numbers."

"That makes no sense to me at all, why would you want to count how many prayers you've said? Do you think it matters to God if you've said something ten times or a hundred times?" Her voice was filled with disdain.

"I don't know, it's more than that. It just reminded me of Father Basil, that's all."

To my relief she dropped the subject but I began to think about him as we ate. As she was clearing away the plates I brought up the subject again. "Would you have any objections if I contacted the monastery and arranged a visit?"

"What, and lose a whole weekend? It's the only time we get nowadays."

"I know, but I wouldn't go for the whole weekend. I can drive over a in a few hours and come back the same day. We could still do something together."

"But why do you want to visit again? You've done that once, what would be the point?"

"You know how much I got from it last time, you said yourself how calm I seemed when I got back. I don't know, I suppose finding the prayer rope has made me think about them again."

"Is everything alright Stewart? Is there something you're not telling me?" The irritation had left her voice and she seemed genuinely concerned.

"No, nothing's wrong, it's not going to be a problem is it?"

"No," she smiled, "you go see your men in black if you must."

The Mini Cooper was old when we bought it, but always started when it needed to and used very little petrol. Father John had answered the telephone and though he had been happy to arrange a day for me to visit, I could sense in his voice that he didn't remember me. As I drove this began to bother me and I realised how my pride had been provoked. I was able to smile at my silliness and the feeling of hurt quickly left me.

Having my own vehicle made the journey much simpler and as I got to about a mile from the monastery I recognised the lanes and began recalling the bus trip the year before. The final half mile of track was much more uneven than I had remembered and fearing for the axles I pulled up where the path was wide enough and set off on foot. This gave me the chance to think a little and I began to plan the questions I might ask Father Basil. There weren't any pressing personal issues I wanted to raise, but I didn't want to turn up without a good reason. The monks had chosen to live away from the world and I knew I shouldn't invade their lives just to satisfy my own vague compunction.

The buildings had been given a fresh coat of paint since my last visit but otherwise everything looked just as I remembered. I approached the front door with more confidence than last time but still I felt a little nervous. I knocked firmly and heard approaching footsteps. The door opened to reveal Father Basil and his smile lifted all the anxiety from me. He kissed me in is usual way and invited me in.

With cups of coffee poured he made himself comfortable opposite me and I noticed that the edges of his beard had begun to turn grey. I looked closely at his face and realised that he was older than I had assumed but his eyes looked as youthful as ever.

"Thank you for letting me visit Father."

"Each time you come it is like the monastery is visited by an angel."

I was slightly caught off guard by this and laughed a little. But I could see he was serious. "Father, a friend raised a question which I was unable to answer."

"Then they are a good friend. We need people like that who make us think a little."

"Yes," I continued, "it was about prayer. I couldn't explain why you use the rope to count off your prayers, when I tried to answer I got it mixed up and didn't really know what to say."

"Well, I am pleased to say you have raised yet another good question for us to think about. And like so many of your questions there are different ways to answer it. First we do not use the rope to count in that sense; we use it so that we do not have to count. By running the rope through our fingers we are able to ignore the counting. If I have chosen to say the Jesus Prayer a hundred times, I can put away thoughts of time and simply work my way along the rope. This way my mind is able to concern itself solely with the task of praying. But I suspect that is only part of what lies behind your question, am I right?"

"Yes Father, why is there a need to keep repeating prayers. Doesn't God hear the first time?"

Now it was Father Basil's turn to laugh. "Yes, God hears everything, spoken and unspoken, but prayer is more than making requests of Him. The words of the Jesus Prayer enable us to focus our whole self on the presence of God. By repeating the words we are able to silence the distractions within us and learn to give our entire attention to God."

"It is so quiet here; I understand why that would help."

"Yes it is a quiet place, and of course that helps. But there are different kinds of silence, both outer and inner. As we work in the vegetable gardens we can enjoy the quiet and beauty of nature, and this is a good thing. But if our minds are racing with worries or thoughts then we might as well be in London. Outward silence is good, but comes and goes, it is temporary. The Jesus prayer is our means to acquiring inner silence. When we have this kind of silence then we can have peace even if we are walking down a crowded London Street. But too few of us have acquired this grace, and so we must seek outer silence to help us on our path to inner silence."

"But if you want silence, why repeat the Jesus Prayer? Isn't that a noise within you?"

"No," he shook his head, "there are different sounds even in the outer world. Some sounds are harmonious and filled with beauty and order, while others are harsh, discordant noises which unsettle us. The same is true of inner sounds. By focussing carefully on the words of the Jesus Prayer we are able to find stillness that is only found in God's presence."

"I'm still not sure about the numbers Father." I felt a little stupid asking. "Why do you have to say particular numbers of prayers?"

"As we grow in the spiritual life we are able to take on greater works. It is not easy at first to keep the mind steady and free of distraction. But with time we learn the discipline of prayer – nothing teaches prayer as much as prayer! So we are able to commit greater periods of the day to prayer. If we try to spend all day in prayer from the very beginning it will be a disaster. Even the holiest Desert Fathers combined times of prayer with work and the singing of psalms. The numbers are really incidental; they are just a way of allowing ourselves a certain amount of time in prayer. Does this make sense to you?"

"Yes," I nodded, "is it a bit like a mantra?"

"No, not at all." He shook his head seriously. "The pagans repeat their phrases to escape the mind, we say the Jesus prayer to fully engage our minds with the living presence of God. The Jesus prayer is not a technique, using the prayer rope isn't a mechanism for achieving results. It is simply a tool which enables us to stay still and focussed. Mantras are about affecting the self, whereas the Jesus Prayer is about meeting with God Who chooses to change us."

"I'm still not sure of the difference," I admitted.

"Mantras are used to transcend this reality, prayer is about engaging fully with this reality because this is where God dwells and meets with us. This is the reality within which God has chosen to give us life; we do not have to escape it. The pagans would have you believe that the body and the entire material world is evil or nothing of value. We do not believe this; our salvation comes in body and soul. This is why all that we do is important; we do not separate off the spiritual self from the physical self in that way."

"Father, you used the word 'works' which I am unsure of."

"What is your understanding of this?" He asked.

"I'm probably wrong, I don't want to caricature what they believe, but don't Roman Catholics believe we are saved through our works and Protestants believe it is by faith alone?"

"There are people amongst those groups who hold those positions, but both ideas are wrong."

"Forgive me Father, but how can they both be wrong? Isn't it one or the other?"

"This false distinction has resulted from the western Reformation, as the two sides of the theological debate sought to define themselves they veered into the extremes of their positions, often in order to make it clear just how different they were from each other. Of course the Church has always had to define its faith when attacked by heresy, and many expressions of the Christian faith have resulted in having to protect the Church from false teachings. But historically the Church has always defined the faith that already is held or professed; it has not created doctrines that are unfamiliar to the faithful in order to make its point. Both Rome and the Protestants have stretched the truth beyond itself in order to show the other to be at fault."

"But how can salvation not be either by works or faith alone, I am still not clear Father?"

"Let us consider each side of this coin in turn. The Protestants would have you believe that faith can exist without works. But the kind of works we are discussing must always accompany faith. Satan believes in God, he knows that Christ is God's Son, he knows judgement day is coming, but such belief does not save him. Faith is not a simple ascent to a particular set of doctrines; it is not enough to profess belief in words. Our Lord warned that on the final day there will be many who indeed called Him Lord but to them He will say "Get away from me, I never knew you." Faith must transform us, it must live in acts of repentance and goodness, it isn't something that exists in the intellect alone but must fill our whole being. Saint James said that "Faith without works is dead". None of us can be saved with a dead faith."

"But that leaves us with works Father; surely what you are saying fits with the Roman Catholic position."

"No, again we must look more closely. First, it is to misunderstand our relationship with God if we think Heaven is a reward for good behaviour. The Fathers teach us that we are not to be like hired hands seeking a reward, we should seek to serve God in gratitude for all that He has done for us. We must see ourselves as unfaithful servants who, even if we spend a lifetime full of great works, must recognise that we have done only that which we should. Heaven is granted by God in love, not as some payment for labours. When we understand how indebted to God we are only then can we begin to understand that there is nothing that we can do worthy of such a great gift. There is simply no work than man is capable of that could earn Heaven."

"But how can we be faithful servants," I asked, "except by works?"

"Christ calls us faithful servants when we do all things in faith."

"That sounds like we're back to salvation by faith," I suggested.

"No, the faith we are speaking about is what drives a man to be obedient to his master. The faithful servant does not toil in order to be rewarded; he serves his master in gratitude and love. The master of a slave is under no obligation to reward the one who has done what is expected of him. God sees the inner workings of each of our hearts; He is not fooled by outward shows but watches the inner man."

"This sounds impossible," I blurted, "how can anyone possibly reach such spiritual heights? Maybe holy monks can be so pure in their motives, but what about the rest of us?"

"Whether we are in or out of the world, God's demands on us are the same. But you must not fear, because our salvation comes from God's mercy. The thief who died beside Christ did not have a lifetime of good works to present in his favour, but our Lord promised him he would be in Paradise that very day. What then did the thief do to earn such a reward? Of course, nothing! But he threw himself on God's mercy, and God accepted him because of his recognition of his sinfulness. The thief acknowledged that he deserved the punishment he was receiving; he did not ask Christ to deliver him from an unjust sentence. We too must not consider ourselves worthy of anything but condemnation, so that when we ask God for mercy He may grant us pardon."

"Is that why the Jesus Prayer asks God for mercy?"

"It is partly in imitation of the thief but it is a different kind of mercy to what might be asked of a judge in court. The Jesus Prayer echoes the call of the crowds who asked for conquering generals to share their spoils of victory. The Jesus Prayer helps us to call on the One Who has conquered all evils, Who has even conquered death. It is a request for the fullness of this victory, which is God's mercy and salvation."

"I think I understand but I am still a little unsure about how we can do this. Isn't it a little presumptuous of us to be grateful for salvation when we don't know if we have received it?"

"Think of the story of the Hebrews and the walls of Jericho. They marched around the city blowing their horns and singing their songs of victory. The songs they sang were a celebration of what they believed God was going to do. It was not the sound of their horns that made the walls tumble down, God responded to their faithfulness. This is how we are to perform our works, not because we believe that they will achieve our salvation, but because in faith we place our trust in God's desire to save us. Remember, His wish for your salvation is infinitely greater than even your own."

He must have recognised an expression of understanding in my face, he smiled and picking up the dirty cups went through to the kitchen. I looked out of the window and saw the fields being buffeted by a strong wind. The house was built of old stone and I knew it could probably withstand a hurricane. Looking at my watch I was surprised to find how much time had passed and I didn't want to be driving for too long in the dark: the little Mini's lights were barely adequate at the best of times. As Father Basil returned I stood and informed him that I needed to be heading back.

"Before you leave we must say a prayer for your journey." He led me out into the cold and we quickly made our way to the church. He held open the door for me and I followed him in. It was a room of shadows in the half light but as Father Basil lit a candle I noticed the movement of the flickering flame dancing as it was reflected in the faces of the saints painted on the walls. I was tired, and as he read a prayer before the iconostasis I began to imagine the saints moving out from the flat painted walls. Instead of a single monk praying alone the room appeared to be full of a crowd of holy figures praying with him. As he finished praying he turned and in the glow of the candlelight his face appeared just like one of the saints in the frescoes. I knew we were surrounded by an invisible company and that they would be praying with me as I drove home.

He led me out and planted the candle in a stand containing sand so that after we had left the light would continue to burn before the images. He then walked with me to the edge of the buildings and thanked me for coming.

"Thank you for letting me have some of your time Father."

"You are welcome any time Stewart, God be with you on your journey." With that he turned and disappeared into the house without looking back. I turned and headed along the lane. The light was fading but despite the conditions I felt content. The Mini was sitting where I had left it; it seemed a strange object in this place. I turned the ignition and felt the usual relief when the engine jumped into life, but I was immediately unsettled by the sound of a rock song blaring out of the radio. I quickly reached down and turned it off, the monastery had left me feeling unable to deal with such intrusion, even the sounds that had entertained me as I had driven here.

I found my way back to the main road and pulled out into the traffic. An endless stream of lights poured past me, strangers off to their own concerns and busy lives. I followed the road signs that guided me mile by mile back to Julie, and in the darkness of my little car I began to mouth the words of the Jesus Prayer: *Lord Jesus Christ, Son of God, have mercy on me a sinner.*

1980

In early 1980 Julie and I were married. We had a little more money coming in and if happiness is possible in this world then we were happy. I hadn't given up hopes of returning to the monastery but mention of the subject usually led to arguments and so I avoided the topic. As close as Julie and I were the difference in our understanding of the Christian faith was widening. Her Baptist roots ran deeper than I had imagined and as we got a little older she retreated slightly to the worldview she had been raised in. My Anglicanism held a much weaker grip on me because by its very nature it could be all things to all men, unless of course you began to question its liberalism. On a day-to-day basis it didn't affect us, we had found a local church which was sufficiently modern to satisfy Julie's taste but which also at least aspired to show some awareness of tradition which was important to me. Of course, the most important factor for us at that time was that the vicar was an impressive man, intelligent and friendly, and his personal charisma was enough to maintain an unusually large congregation at a time when other local parishes were shrinking.

Our first few months together were a real blessing and it wasn't until Easter of that first year that I realised there could be a problem. I had been reading a number of books about the early Church and as my understanding grew I began to have questions for which I couldn't find the answers. The vicar had an impressive knowledge of post-Reformation theologians, but he seemed to think that Church history stopped with the writing of the New Testament and kicked in again in the sixteenth century. He would sometimes refer to the "dark ages" but I knew there were countless spiritual giants who had lived during that period and that in the East it had been far from dark.

The Easter Sunday service brought things out into the open. It was a lively affair and the vicar's teenage son had been given permission to lead the music group with his electric guitar. Between verses he let loose with short solos which were greeted with excited clapping and the place took on the air of a rock concert. As we sang our way through a hymn which had the subtlety of a primary school poem a few people began to lift their hands in the air in response to the stirring of their emotions. I had felt something similar when I had seen my favourite band perform; I knew it had nothing to do with God.

As we drove away from the church it was clear that Julie's enthusiasm had not yet subsided and I tried to avoid conversation that might lead to confrontation. But she was determined to talk about it. "What did you think of the service?" She asked.

"People seemed to be having a good time," was all I could manage.

"Yea, there was a good vibe, it felt like a Baptist church."

"I know what you mean," I said, "not a typical C. of E. do."

"Did you enjoy it?" The bluntness of her question didn't allow me to wriggle out of answering, but I was still trying to be diplomatic.

"It wasn't really my thing if I'm honest Julie."

"Why not?"

"It doesn't matter, I just wasn't into it."

"How can you not be into it?" Her voice hinted at anger.

"Why would that bother you? If you enjoyed it then fair enough."

"I suppose there weren't enough icons for your taste!" Anger was now fueling her reaction and her tone sufficiently irritated me that avoiding an argument no longer mattered.

"It's got nothing to do with that. If you really want to know I thought the whole thing was awful. The music was horrible; those hymns belong in nursery school...it felt manipulative."

"Manipulative!" The word sounded more serious when she said it and I knew I had gone too far. "How the hell was it manipulative? Who's being manipulative? What a bizarre thing to say."

"No, I'm not saying it was deliberately manipulative, but didn't you think it was winding people's emotions up?"

"Yes, that's what it's supposed to do," her anger was now in control of her.

"Do you mean worship? Do you really think worship is meant to get you into an emotional state?" My voice had become calm; I was genuinely interested to hear what she had to say.

"Worship is about the whole person, aren't your emotions part of that? You can't turn off that part of yourself when you meet with God. Read your Old Testament, King David danced around plenty enough."

"It's not what we see when we look at the first Christians. Saint Paul warned them to keep good order; the early Church's worship was liturgical, not tambourines and guitars."

"You haven't answered my question," she was also more controlled now, "how is it manipulative?"

"I've seen people get themselves into a state like that over all sorts of things. I've felt it when I've been to concerts; it's what can happen when you get crowds of people together. Look at those political rallies in America, or the way the crowds reacted to Hitler."

"So you're comparing the service to a Nazi rally now! Unbelievable." She turned her head away and looked out the window.

"No, of course I'm not. I'm just saying that people's emotions can be brought out by certain kinds of music or atmosphere. "

She turned back to me, "Okay, bottom line, do you think it was the Holy Spirit that people were experiencing?" Her question felt dangerous.

"No, I think it was a group dynamic. I don't think it had anything to do with God." She had pushed me into a corner and I had said more than I wanted, but with the statement out I knew I believed it.

She shook her head; I could see she was shocked. "And you think the same goes for Baptist services?"

I hesitated, she was going to take anything I said as a judgment on her self, but she had pushed enough that I felt vindicated. "Yes I do."

"This is unbelievable," she nearly spat the words, "it's just so insulting."

"I'm sorry Julie, I'm not trying to be insulting. Do you want me to pretend?"

"Of course I don't, but it would be nice if you didn't think my entire church tradition was based on hysteria."

"That's not what I'm saying..."

"So what are you saying Stewart?"

"I don't know, I'm sorry."

We fell into silence for the rest of the journey and once home we put some distance between our selves and found various jobs to occupy our time. Later that evening I found her watching television and sat beside her.

"You okay?" I asked.

She gave me a warm smile and slid her arms around me. I pulled her closer and it was a relief to know the anger had passed. But anxiety filled me again when she said "Do you think the Baptist Church is really the Church?"

The experience from earlier had me wary of saying too much, and she sensed my uncertainty.

"It's okay," she assured me, "I'm not looking for another fight. I just want to know."

Her tone convinced me that she wanted honesty. "I don't know Julie, I'm just not sure."

"What about the Anglican Church?" She kept pushing.

"Same answer, I don't know."

She thought for a moment, "If you don't know, is that a problem?"

I pulled my arm from around her shoulder and leaned forward, "If we have children it will be very important. Don't you have to be absolutely sure that you're part of God's Church?"

"I am," she replied, "I have faith and I participate in worship. I don't have any insecurity about whether I'm in or out."

"I don't know Julie," I repeated, "and it's important to be sure. If I've got any doubts then I need to look at them."

"Do you mean doubts about God?"

"No, not those kinds of doubts, doubts about who the Church is and whether I'm part of it. One thing I do know is that I can't not be sure. When we have kids, I have to be certain that they're members of the Church and if I have any doubts then they have to be addressed. It's too important to take any chances. Does that make sense?"

She pulled closer again, talk of children softened her attitude to me and I knew she was enjoying talking about the future in this way. I decided to seize the moment, "How would you feel about me visiting the monastery soon?"

I felt her stiffen slightly, but her voice was still tender. "Do you really have to run back to your monks whenever you can't figure something out?"

"It's been nearly three years," I protested, "I wouldn't call that always running back to them." I gave her a gentle squeeze as she thought about things.

"I don't have the right to stop you Stewart, and it's wrong of me to make you feel bad about wanting to go. I'm sorry, of course you should go, but don't stay overnight."

"I won't, I promise, I'll give them a ring in a few days."

It felt good to have her agreement and as we sat in front of the television for the rest of the night my thoughts began turning once more to Brother Basil and the monastery on the hillside.

I was driving a better car and carrying the first hints of extra weight around my middle, but as I got to within a few miles of the monastery I felt the same excitement I had experienced the first time I had made the trip. I looked out for the same pull-in I had left the Mini in and this small moment of familiarity gave me confidence. I strode quickly along the last stretch of muddy lane and as I finally caught sight of the monastery buildings it didn't seem possible that so much time had elapsed since my last visit.

The afternoon sunshine felt warm in my face and as I approached the front door I found a long black cat stretched out on the doorstep. He was oblivious to me as I drew near, and I stopped to enjoy the sight of him sunning himself. When I leaned forward and knocked at the door the cat rolled over in a very leisurely manner and began stretching its legs. It moved over to me and began to purr as it rubbed its head and neck against my leg. I bent down to stroke him and it was in this pose that Father Basil found me as he opened the door.

"I see the new member of the monastery is making herself known to you."

"It's a she; I didn't think you were allowed any female animals in a monastery."

"That's not strictly true; they don't keep female animals on Athos, with the exception of cats." He kissed my cheek and patted my shoulder affectionately. "They are the one animal that can take care of themselves when they give birth, so there is no risk of them interrupting a monk's cycle of prayer." He grinned as he looked down at her, "and she is a good servant to the monastery. Don't let her easy-going manner fool you, at night she works hard keeping out unwanted visitors. She is a first class mouse catcher and keeps long vigils."

The cat looked up at me and casually sauntered off to find a quieter place to enjoy the sun.

"It has been a long time Stewart, how are you?" I briefly described to him the little matters that filled my days and he was pleased to hear about the wedding. The few years since I last saw him had left their mark on his appearance. His already sunken cheeks now barely hid the bones of his skull and around his eyes were heavy rings. His beard had turned the colour of blue steel from the blend of black and grey hairs and I knew that he would be able to see a different effect that time had had on me. He explained that he was alone in the monastery while the other monks visited Mount Athos.

"Is everything alright at home Stewart? Married life is not always an easy adjustment to make."

"Yes, we're happy together Father, we're still enjoying the honeymoon period."

"Good, and what about other things?"

I wasn't sure if he was talking about my work or if he was inviting me to touch on the reason I had come. "There have been things on my mind Father."

"Please, go ahead." He nodded encouragement.

"How can I be sure if I am part of the Church?"

"Your question implies that you feel uncertain Stewart."

"I am, I don't know what to think. When I read the Church Fathers they seem so clear that you either belong to the Church or you don't."

"We live in a different age, in some ways the matter is more complicated for us, but in other ways it is unchanged."

This sounded a little cryptic to me, I wanted a straight answer. "I'm not sure what you mean."

"For a thousand years there was one Orthodox Church, heretics were seen to be outside of it, and every member of the Church was in communion with the others. The Church shared one faith, one baptism and one cup. In such a world it was easy to draw clear distinctions between who was part of the Church and who was outside it."

"But if that was true then," I insisted, "surely it must be the case now. Aren't these things eternal?"

"Yes, they are. But when the Roman Patriarch left communion with the rest of the Church there existed a second body who claimed to be the Church. In reality there can only be one Church in the world, Christ did not establish many churches at Pentecost, it was the same Church founded that spread to Corinth and Jerusalem and Rome. This split was not simply a human debate that had got out of hand, East and West believed different things about God and the Church, there were fundamental differences that meant that the two sides could not share communion."

"I have read about the Great Schism Father, but I can't get to the bottom of the *filioque*. Why would that one word cause so many problems?"

"When the western churches changed the symbol of faith, the Creed, by adding this Latin word 'filioque', they changed their understanding of God. It translates as "and from the Son". Rome introduced the belief that the Holy Spirit proceeds not just from the Father but also from the Son. This reduces the status of the Holy Spirit within the

Holy Trinity, it changes the nature of God and consequently demotes the status of the Church since it is the Holy Spirit alive in us that makes us the Body."

"If the western church started believing in heresy, doesn't that mean they are no longer part of the Church?"

"This is where we must tread carefully. It is absolutely true that there can be no place for such heretical teaching in God's Church, and those who profess such faith must repent of their error in order to be received back into the Church. But I do not wish to appear harsh, it is not my place to say who is righteous before God and who is not. There are some Orthodox thinkers who believe that the edge of the Church's existence is blurred and that it is impossible for any of us to say who is not part of the Church. We can only say with certainty who is part of the Body, and that is those members of the Apostolic Church who participate in her sacramental life with faith."

"What about those Christians who are very devout but belong to other denominations?"

"These other Christian societies have elements of the truth, but not the fullness of truth. We must pray that in His mercy God will work through what truth they have to reach them. And clearly He does, there are many, very sincere Christians I have met who belong to different church groups. You yourself have a thirst for God which is nourished by what you have found outside the Church."

These were difficult words to hear, partly because they confronted my position and partly because I knew they were true. "Does the depth of faith a person has count for nothing Father?"

"Of course a strong faith is a great blessing and is very important. But we must be careful how we look at this, we are living in confused times and it is hard for us to see clearly. The West has become a very individualised society, man has raised the status of "self" to the level of an idol. In America the idea of personalised faith is rampant. We feel ourselves living as individuals within our communities, our sense of connection and belonging is withering. Yes our personal faith is important, but belonging to the Church is far more than this. We do not become the Church just because of a personal declaration of faith. The Church must act in response to our faith, it has authority from God to bring people into the Church through the sacraments of Baptism and Chrismation. And that new life is then sustained by the other sacraments, it is an ongoing journey that we make, not a once and for all event that guarantees salvation. Think about the Apostles. They saw Christ crucified and encountered Him after His resurrection. They spoke with Him, witnessed Him eating and drinking. And yet this did not make them the Church. Their belief was unquestionable, they saw with their own eyes Christ resurrected: but to be the Church something more was needed. The descent of the Holy Spirit changed them, The Church is not simply a gathering of people who share particular beliefs. It is a mystical Body created and sustained by the Holy Spirit." He paused for a moment, and then added "Even membership of the Church is far from being a guarantee of salvation. The Church is the hospital to which we must turn for treatment of the sickness of our soul, and while we receive the sacramental care we always remember that we are sick. The Church is the means through which God heals us. Of course God acts in other ways, but He has chosen this specific means of giving us His grace."

A part of me needed to hear this said, it confirmed a realisation I had been moving towards for some time. I decided to ask what was for me the burning question: "Do the sacraments of the other denominations save us?"

His face was serious, "It has always been the belief of the Church that there can be no salvic action in anything called sacraments outside the Church. There has always been some debate about whether converts should be re-baptised, but beyond this it is very clear. The Holy Spirit brought the Church into being, and the authority of the Church does not extend to heretics."

"Why is what we believe so important Father, doesn't God look beyond the content of belief to the state of the heart?"

"The heart is where faith lives. Your question is another product of this modern idea of the self. We grow up encouraged to think whatever we like as though it has no consequence. But from the very beginning it has always been the understanding of the Church that right belief is as much a moral issue as right action. On judgement day we will be held to account not just for what we have done and said, but for what we think and believe. It is one thing to be in error, but a heretic is one who rejects correction and wilfully persists in his error. It is a very serious sin."

"What about people born in parts of the world where they have never known the faith? What about people born in countries where they are raised in a different faith?"

"God's mercy and love extends to all people everywhere. God can reach the heart of a man who is a pagan through the little truth his religion teaches. God can speak to a native in the Amazonian jungle through the beauty and order of creation. God's truth is everywhere and we are created to respond to Him however far we walk from the fullness of truth."

Father Basil understood where this conversation was guiding me, and also my motivation for raising the questions. A difficult decision lay ahead of me and I had no idea how I was going to explain things to Julie.

"You must pray for your wife, God will make all things possible." He spoke to my heart despite the outward confusion I seemed to be in. We had reached a point where more words weren't necessary and he invited me to join him to see the new building under construction at the rear of the monastery. The sun was still high over our heads and the cat had found some shade beside a wall. She opened her eyes as we passed but made no attempt to move.

The building work was at an early stage, foundations were dug and a few carefully piled bricks sat waiting to be used.

"We are building a larger guest house, you will be more comfortable if you stay over night."

"Do you get many people coming to the monastery?"

"Quite a few in the summer and around certain feasts. There are many people in the world who need some time here to reflect or like you, ask questions. We have had to turn people away for lack of space. We are doing most of the work ourselves but will bring in an electrician to do the wiring."

It was a relief to know that I wasn't the only one who invaded their life here and the construction work felt like a positive sign, it reassured me that the monks didn't object to us coming.

"The monastery grows in bricks and mortar," he said thoughtfully, "and soon it will grow in other ways."

His eyes were fixed on something I couldn't perceive, and though he spoke of something beyond my vision, I trusted that his words were true.

Julie greeted my return with lots of affection but didn't ask about my trip beyond enquiries about the roads and whether Father Basil was in good health. I wanted to talk through many things but raising the topics and being asked about them was very different. Once more I quickly found myself slipping back into the routine of normal life but again the sense of change in me was growing. One night after we had eaten Julie finally started raising questions that we both knew she had been preparing.

"Did you get the answers you were looking for at the monastery?" She seemed genuinely interested.

"Yes, in a way, but I wouldn't say things are resolved."

"What's not resolved Stewart?"

"You know, issues to do with the Church."

"So where does that leave you now? Or should I say, where does that leave us?"

"What do you mean? How does it affect us?"

"If you're moving towards Orthodoxy I'm afraid I won't be coming with you. I'm perfectly happy where I am. I just don't see why you have to leave the traditions you've been brought up in."

"That's just it," I said, "the Church of England isn't even the Church I knew as a kid. It's changing all the time, new morals, new attitudes to lots of things. If we bring our kids up as Anglicans we'll have no idea what it will look like in ten years, let alone twenty or thirty."

"Then why don't we start worshipping with the Baptists, you know I'm happy there."

"I can't do that Julie, I'm sorry, but I'm not having my children pushed out into the world unbaptised. You don't want that either."

She hesitated at this, it was the one issue within her old tradition that she struggled with. "But do you want your children growing up with parents that can't even worship in the same place together?" Her question carried no ill intent, I could see the concern she was genuinely feeling.

"No, I don't want that." And as I spoke the words I knew I meant them. We had reached a point where I could see no way forward. Everything I was coming to believe, all that I understood as truth was pulling me in a different direction to that of my longing to make my wife happy and maintain an untroubled home. Perhaps if we had been married longer and I had felt more secure in our union I might have made different choices, but holding her close to me I wanted nothing more at that moment than to love her and be loved by her: anything that felt like a threat to this was unwelcome and in my human frailty I consciously chose to ignore what I believed God was saying to me.

1984

I allowed three and a half years to slip by. Father Basil responded to my occasional letters, but in them I avoided saying anything important. I tried to convince myself that the issues had been settled, and I found ways of thinking about the Church that enabled me to side-step what I knew to be true. The worst part of this was when I was praying. Every time I turned to God I knew I was ignoring His voice, or even worse, I was trying to shout over it so loudly that I could pretend it wasn't there. I quickly learned how easy it is to turn away from God, even when we are going through the motions of a Christian life. As we grew out of our youth our faith took on an increasing importance. We were now regulars at our local parish church, we briefly prayed together every day, and I continued to consume Christian literature at a hungry pace. Outwardly I was doing what I thought was right, but the inner sense of disobedience created a discomfort that was turning my heart hollow within me. I managed to pull off this prolonged act of stupidity for one reason alone: Julie was a wonderful wife and the happiness she brought me gave me enough to cling to. Marriage suited us and we sensed that God had blessed us deeply. But I was able to twist this into a conviction that since God had allowed us to be so content then He couldn't really want me to risk upsetting things.

Our first child arrived in late 1983, we named him James, and it seemed our blessings would never end. We felt no immediate rush to get our son baptised but once the New Year had passed we made arrangements with our vicar and set a date. Julie was now as firmly convinced about infant baptism as I was but I knew she had had to face one or two difficult questions from members of her family. A good crowd of family and friends arrived on the day of the service, so many in fact that we nearly doubled the size of the congregation. The vicar had invited us to choose a few of our favourite hymns and Julie had taken the opportunity to make a selection that would meet with her family's approval.

All was going well, the godparents made their responses with appropriate enthusiasm, and our son was taking it all in without a murmur. At the font we handed him over to the vicar who repeated the prayers and held him over the water. But instead of pouring water over his head in the name of the Holy Trinity, the vicar dipped his finger into the water and drew a cross on the baby's forehead. Julie and I looked at each other; she hid her concern far less than me: a deep frown appeared above her eyes. She looked round at her parents who stared back at her with a "we told you so" expression. We said nothing of course, and returned to our pews to endure the rest of the service. I felt my stomach tightening; I had no idea what to do. I needed to object, ask for assurance, do anything that could calm my confusion. Only when we were passed the vicar's greeting at the door were we able to share a few words.

"I can't believe what I've just seen," said Julie. "That wasn't a baptism Stewart."

"I know," I assured her, "we'll talk about it later. Let's not do it now."

As my parents approached to make a fuss of their grandson Julie nodded and it was a relief to shield ourselves from our anxiety with the social niceties of hosting a party. Even Julie's parents seemed to have accepted that this must be the way they do it in the Church of England and weren't pushing for an explanation. But I had witnessed plenty of Anglican baptisms where the child at least got wet; I knew this wasn't the norm even for the liberal end of Protestantism.

Our concerns didn't prevent us from enjoying the party and when the guests had headed off on their journeys home we were left feeling happy to have shown off our son. The day had worn him out and Julie settled him down early. She found me listening to music and sat close to me on the couch.

"Was that a baptism Stewart?"

"I don't know," I admitted, "I don't know what to think."

"I may not be Baptist when it comes to everything, but I know there has to be water involved. He barely wet his finger; there was nothing to dry with the towel when he handed

James back to me. That's just not right." Her eyes were filling with tears as she spoke.

"I don't know what to say. I've never seen anything like it."

"Do you think we should ring him up and tell him what we think?" There was desperation in her voice.

I hesitated, "What would be the point? If he thinks he's doing baptisms like that he must believe it's okay. What can we tell him?"

"We need to speak to someone, what if we go to the Archdeacon?"

"To do what? He's not going to do the baptism again for us, and it'll just look like we're trying to cause trouble."

"We can't just leave it Stewart, not if you really believe baptism is important."

I nodded, but I didn't say what I was thinking. There was someone I wanted to speak to but Julie was already troubled enough without raising Father Basil's name. Which was why I was shocked when Julie said "You should write to the monastery. Ask them for some advice. Tell them exactly what's happened and ask them straight up if we can be confident about this baptism. I've got to know Stewart, this is horrible."

I held her tightly; it was a comfort to be speaking so openly without it creating conflict.

"I'll write to them this week," I promised.

"No," she was adamant, "do it tonight. Don't go to bed until it's written, I'll post it for you tomorrow."

I did as I was told. Just as it had been a relief to speak freely with Julie, it was equally liberating to be writing to Father Basil and be able to pour out what was in my heart. As I began to write it was as though I were sitting once again at his table and all my struggles and fears began to appear on the page. As I wrote I found myself being as honest with myself as I was with him, and for the first time since I had seen him I consciously knew that God was calling us to be Orthodox. But instead of the anxiety and uncertainty it had once raised, a calm joy now filled me and I experienced a peace I had denied myself for nearly four years. I finally accepted it, and immediately I felt a reassurance that we were doing the right thing.

When I had finished writing I took it to the bedroom where Julie was reading. I offered her the letter and she quietly read through the lines that I had been unable to express directly to her. I could feel my heart beating nervously as I waited, but when she looked up her face broke into a smile.

"I know this is how you've been feeling," she said gently, "I'm not there yet, but I understand."

About a week after sending our letter we received Father Basil's response. Even holding the unopened envelope affected me: knowing he had focussed his attention on these sheets of paper for us was reassuring even before I had read his words. It felt like a tangible sign that we were still connected with something beyond our present circumstances, a sign of hope. I took great care tearing the envelope and sat at my desk to read it.

Dear Stewart,

I am sorry to read of your concerns about the baptism of your son. I will try to answer your questions as best as I am able. You are right when you say that water must be poured over the head at baptism, it is one of the necessary signs of the sacrament. When converts are received into Orthodoxy the previous baptism may be considered acceptable only when it is known that sufficient water was used. In the case of your son a priest would certainly insist that the baptism be performed properly before chrismation could take place. Do not allow yourself to feel panic about this, I sensed in your letter how upset you are about it. All will happen in God's time, your task is simply to be obedient to what you believe God is saying to you.

You asked me if I thought you were sinning by not yet seeking Orthodoxy. I cannot answer that question for you, but I do think it suggests that you yourself know whether God is calling you to seek it. It is sometimes advisable not to rush into such decisions, but I would say you have given yourself a good length of time to make a decision.

I am glad to hear Julie is well and that she is supportive of your feelings about Orthodoxy. My suggestion now would be to find yourself an Orthodox parish where you can experience worship and the ongoing life of the Church. I enclose a list of priests' addresses that are within travelling distance for you. As you can see there is nothing within fifty miles of where you live, so you are going to have to commit yourself to a little driving in order to find the parish that suits you. I should warn you that the liturgies will be in Greek or Slavonic, and that the congregations will be made up of ethnic Orthodox. It may be something of a curiosity for them to have an Englishman turn up to their services – don't let their reactions put you off in any way. Give the priest a telephone call before you go, it will make things easier.

Pray that God will lead you to the right parish. And pray for me and all here at the monastery.

*Yours in Christ,
the sinful monk, Basil.*

I re-read it a couple of times and then found Julie in the kitchen. I took over baby-sitting duties while she disappeared to read the letter. As I played with James I found myself feeling confident about his future. I was determined that he was going to grow up within the unshakeable framework of the Church and nothing the world could throw at us could rob us of what this meant. Eventually Julie returned looking very sombre.

"I need some time to think about this Stewart. I'm glad he's confirmed what we were already thinking about the baptism – at least we know it's not just us being awkward. But I don't know how I feel about having to travel all that way to get to church. What if we can't speak to any one? How will we ever fit in? I need that sense of community."

"I know, I feel the same. But God will take care of us if it's the right thing to do. We've just got to trust in Him."

She nodded, "Okay."

I gave her the broadest smile that my face could manage, "Thank you."

The following evening I rang the number of the parish closest to us. A heavily accented man's voice answered but it wasn't the priest. I tried to explain that I wished to attend worship with them and asked about the time of the Liturgy. Amongst a lot of words that made little sense I gathered it was a 10 am. start and thanked him for his help. I wasn't entirely confident that he had understood what I was asking but resolved to make the trip that weekend. Julie was happy to let me make this first visit alone and I found my mind wandering in anticipation through out the rest of the week.

I set off at eight on Sunday morning and the empty roads meant I made the journey in good time. The church was a converted Methodist chapel and from the outside the only hint of something other than English Protestantism was the notice board in Greek. The car park was nearly full and my Rover looked decidedly shabby next to the BMWs and four wheel drives – some of these Greeks were clearly doing okay for themselves. I made my way round to the front of the building where two Greek ladies were loudly talking. They ignored my attempt at "good morning" but watched as I tried to push open the door. My senses were hit immediately as clouds of sweet smelling incense filled my nostrils. A choir was singing in the balcony above me, their voices blending perfectly. I was deeply struck by the beauty of the hymn despite not understanding the words.

The pews had been removed and instead the congregation of about sixty people stood facing the intricately painted iconostasis. A few turned to look at me as I entered, but most were focussed on the icons before them. As the choir stopped singing the priest's voice began to chant prayers in Greek to which the whole congregation responded. His voice was deep and resonant and conveyed a seriousness that left no doubt about the importance of what was taking place. I found a place at the back next to another old lay dressed in black, her eyes perpetually focussed on the floor before her. In her hands was a prayer rope which she moved slowly as the Liturgy progressed.

The priest emerged to cense us and the clouds of smoke gave shape to the shafts of sunlight streaming through the high windows. There was no organ accompaniment; the service was expressed entirely in human voice. There was something powerful about this, the worship came directly from human beings and I could see and hear an offering to God that was beyond any point in time. It was as though earth and heaven were touching; everyone present had stepped out of time, only the worship of God mattered at that moment and it was as though every mind and heart present was attempting to focus entirely on that one purpose.

I couldn't speak the language and the form of the Liturgy was entirely unknown to me, but I knew that I was experiencing what was right and true. It was impossible to rationalise it but I had an overpowering sense of belonging. Not to that particular group of people or that specific place, but I knew that what was happening was part of something beyond what could be seen. Here was worship that overlapped with what was being offered in Heaven, like the first chamber of a great building through which one must pass to meet the king. I had never before had such a profound sense of people participating in the activity of angels.

Towards the end of the service I watched as a line formed to receive communion. At the head of the queue were the children who received reverently as full members of what was taking place. They weren't the Church of the future or the Church in waiting; they were simply the younger members of the Church here and now. There was nothing sentimental about the way they participated, and it was clear that they knew they were as much a part of this as anyone else. I thought about my own son for a moment, and knew I wanted this for him.

As things came to an end the priest appeared once more with a large basket of bread. As the congregation lined up to receive their final blessing the old lady beside me took my arm and began guiding me toward the back of the queue. I protested and tried to explain that I wasn't Orthodox but she wasn't about to let go of me. A younger woman gave me an assuring smile and I made my way forward as each person received their bread in turn. I found myself standing before the priest who held out a large piece of blessed bread. Unsure of what I should say I received it and thanked him. I found my way back to my place of safety and began chewing on the crust. A tray of coffee cups appeared and some of the ladies began handing them round. To my relief I went unnoticed and after a little while managed to slip out without having to explain my presence. I wasn't ready to start answering questions about why I was there and conversation would have interfered with the picture I was painting in my mind for Julie.

As I climbed into my car I felt elated but then I began to imagine all kinds of possible difficulties. I knew that Julie would need to connect with other members of the congregation and I was concerned that we would forever be outsiders in a parish where we couldn't speak the language. As I tried to think of a way round this I realised I was worrying about things that hadn't yet come to pass and I managed to let go of the anxiety. Immediately a sense of peace took over and I knew that this day was an important step towards something that lay ahead of us. There are times when we perceive meaning even when it has no obvious cause or reason. This was a moment filled with meaning, like an artist's first brush stroke on a blank canvass.

That evening Julie listened to my excited account of the day and seemed genuinely happy that it had gone so well. She wasn't willing to commit herself to making the trip just yet, but I could see it would happen. In fact it was another two months before she agreed to finally visit the parish. By then I had been three times and each time was greeted with a little more familiarity. I still hadn't spoken to the priest and so suggested that we contact him before Julie's visit but she preferred to take a look without officially declaring who we were.

We drove down as a family and I tried to prepare her as best I could. My nervousness irritated her and she told me to let her make her own mind up without my prepping. I needn't have worried. Having a small child in her arms made Julie an instant centre of attention. The older Greek ladies fussed around her and through their broken English made her feel very welcome. They seemed to view me with a little less suspicion now that they could see I had a family and I was made to feel more at home than on any of my previous visits.

The Liturgy was as beautiful as ever and I kept glancing across at Julie to judge her reactions but it was impossible to tell how she felt. After the service we were offered coffee and a young man in his twenties introduced himself to us.

"Hello," he said, "I am Gregory, I have seen you before. Are you Orthodox?"

"No," I said, "we are just visiting." I would have answered differently if I had been alone, but then to my surprise Julie added "We are considering becoming Orthodox."

"Good, I am happy for you," said Gregory, "it is a great blessing to be Orthodox."

"You sound English," I said, "were you raised Orthodox?"

"Oh yes, my parents are from Cyprus but I was born in London. I am English, but I am Orthodox first." He smiled at this. "How did you hear about us?"

"Through a monk called Father Basil," I explained.

"I know Father Basil very well; I was at the monastery only last month. He is a holy man," he paused for a moment, "I think he is a living saint."

Julie didn't react to this comment but I was happy to hear someone else speak so highly of Father Basil. I hadn't consciously thought those words but I immediately agreed with them.

"It was Father Basil who suggested your parish to us," I said.

We chatted over our coffee for a while and then Julie insisted it was time we headed back. As we walked across the car park she took my hand and the gesture confirmed everything I had hoped for. James was still asleep as I strapped his seat into the back and we headed for home.

"You should ring the priest when we get home," she said, "unless you want to go and visit one of the other parishes first."

"I'll ring him, I don't think there's any need to look at the others."

Much of the journey passed in silence, but eventually Julie said "I think I'd like to visit the monastery some time. Do you think that'd be alright?"

"I don't know," I admitted, "I can ring and ask. I don't know what the rules are about women."

We returned to a week of work and domestic life and said very little about what had happened. It was as though we knew there was no need to say too much, our task now was to be patient. We had copied the priest's telephone number from the church notice board and discovered that it was different to the one Father Basil had given me. As the receiver was lifted at the other end I said "Hello, is that Father Philotheos?"

"Yes, how can I help you?" His voice carried only a hint of an accent.

"I've bee coming to your services over the past few months and I wondered if I could come and speak to you some time."

"Are you Orthodox?" That same question kept popping up.

"No Father, not yet."

We arranged a time on the following Saturday and I thanked him for agreeing to see us. Julie showed no reaction to the news and for the rest of the evening remained quite thoughtful and preoccupied. When Saturday finally arrived we drove over without James, Julie's sister was staying with us and it was agreed that he was better off at home. Father Philotheos' house was a typical semi-detached building that in no way stood out from any of the others on the street. I wasn't really aware of what I was expecting but the normality of his home did surprise me. He appeared at the door in his black rassa (cassock), his greying hair tied back in a knot at the back of his head. He welcomed us in and led us to an extension at the back of the house that had been converted into an office. The walls were adorned with icons and the air carried the smell of incense that had been burned a few hours before. He invited us to sit and offered us tea. He then disappeared for a few minutes and when he returned he assured us that it was on its way. While we had his office to ourselves I read some of the titles on his book shelves and found a mixture of Greek and English authors.

On his return he calmly sat opposite us and said "You are wanting to become Orthodox?" His question was blunt and required a straight forward response. I looked at Julie who, without looking back at me said "Yes."

"Why?" At this question Julie glanced over at me, a gesture inviting me to answer.

I turned to him and said "We have been thinking about it for a few years. We have come to the conclusion that there can only be one Church in the world and that the Orthodox Church is it."

He paused for a moment, and to my disappointment said "If you can, you should stay where you are."

I wasn't sure how to respond, it wasn't what I had expected to hear. But Julie stepped in, "We can't remain Anglican."

"What is it about Anglicanism that you don't like?" He asked.

"It isn't a reaction against Anglicanism," said Julie, "we just think our home is in Orthodoxy."

He shook his head. "The Anglican Church is a good organisation, it has many fine priests. This is the church of your nation; you should try to belong to it. Why do you feel the need to go looking elsewhere?"

"Please Father, we have become convinced of the truth of Orthodoxy," I was almost pleading, "we believe it is God's will for us."

He pulled a face, "It is too easy to leave and join churches in the West. It is harder to join your local golf club than it is to become a Methodist or an Anglican. Becoming Orthodox is not like joining the Rotary Club. It takes time; a year of learning and only then if the Church believes you are serious can you convert."

He paused for a moment, watching our reactions to be sure we had taken in what he was saying.

"And make no mistake, it is a conversion. If you become a Baptist or a Methodist your friends will not think anything of it. Even if you become Roman Catholic people will understand. But becoming Orthodox is something different; no one will understand what you have done. It will seem strange, it will create many difficulties. And God will test your desire many times. God will ask you if you really want Him, He will make it hard for you. Are you sure you are willing to face all of this?"

Julie spoke up again, "I don't know if we are strong enough, but I do know that if it's what God wants then He will give us the strength to face it."

Father Philotheos looked at her with a serious expression, but before he could respond the door opened and his wife came in carrying a tray of tea cups. She was a small, dark haired woman whose smile relieved the tension we were feeling.

"This is Stewart and Julie," said Father Philotheos, "they are going to become Orthodox."

1985

During the following year we attended the Liturgy as a family once each month and I made the trip by myself on at least one other Sunday between. On those days when Julie was with me Father Philotheos would invite us to his house where he would spend around an hour each time teaching us the basics of Orthodoxy. I had assumed my previous reading had given me a good understanding of the Orthodox faith but I quickly discovered that I had barely dipped my toe in the ocean. The cool response he had initially given us was quickly replaced with a warmth and care that made us feel very welcome. Our Sunday expeditions took most of the day but when we were tempted to complain we remembered that Father Philotheos was giving us his time after serving the Liturgy and we overcame our self-pity.

The more we learned the more we knew we were making the right decision. Everything about Orthodoxy made sense to us, and as we discovered more, the conviction was only reinforced. The theological in-fighting of Protestantism had been a terrible distraction, and while we had been caught up in defending the most basic doctrines of faith against liberal heresies we had been prevented from moving forwards. As Orthodoxy has spread through the western world there have been competing claims to authority over territory amongst some bishops, and in this early stage of conversion there have been human disputes. But we really didn't care about any of this, we had no nationalistic or ethnic concerns mixed in with our faith, all that mattered was that here was a Church where a shared faith was the basis of everything. If an Orthodox bishop began teaching heresy the people would reject him, there simply is no room for deviation from the truth. This was all that mattered to us, we were comforted to know that the ancient belief of the Apostles was still to be found unadulterated in the twentieth century.

After ten months of being catechumens Father Philotheos finally set a date for us to be received: it would be on the feast of the Raising of Lazarus. The symbolism was not lost on us. We had been so focussed on visiting the parish that thoughts about visiting the monastery had been dropped and so I was surprised when, as we drove back that Sunday afternoon Julie raised the topic once more. "Do you think we could arrange a visit to see Father Basil before we are received?"

"I think so, if he's around," I said, "why, is there something you want to raise with him?"

"No, I just think it would be a good idea. If there were any issues I'd ask Father Philotheos."

"I'll give him a ring tonight," I promised, "I'd like to see him again too."

Any concerns we had about Julie visiting the monastery were brushed aside. It was good to hear his voice again on the telephone and its familiarity made me realise how much time had passed since I had last visited. But I was happy to speak to him now that I was no longer running away from what I knew God wanted of us.

We set off on the following Saturday morning; we had tried to arrange for Julie's sister to take care of James but had ended up strapping him into the back of the car once more. The sense of excitement returned as I drove along the familiar roads but Julie seemed preoccupied. I left her to her thoughts and with James fast asleep enjoyed the chance to recall memories of the monastery. We made good time and lifting my still sleeping son over my shoulder we began the last stretch on foot. The entrance had been rebuilt with a large archway which was now adorned with angels either side of a much larger cross.

Father Basil answered the sound of our knock at the door and even as I held James he threw his arms around me and kissed my cheeks. The joy of his welcome was infectious and I turned to see Julie smiling broadly.

"Julie," said Father Basil, "it has been a long time since the university. Welcome to the monastery."

"Thank you Father, it's good to finally be here."

He gently stroked the head of our sleeping son and invited us in. At his offer of coffee Julie requested tea which for some reason annoyed me. I threw her a look which she shrugged off.

On his return he asked about our lives and we eagerly told him about our experiences with Father

Philotheos. He listened carefully and shared in our happiness when we told him about our approaching reception.

"It is a great blessing for all of you," he said, "there will be many joys but also many struggles ahead. You will find that there is a very real difference when you receive Holy Communion, and you may experience other changes when you are chrismated. For some people God gives a blast of His grace as a sign of reassurance, but be prepared for temptations too. What you are doing is pleasing to God, but the demons will attack you. Do not be alarmed at this, they cannot do anything that God does not permit. But God wants strong warriors in His army, and you can only grow strong when you are tested. This is a blessing for you as a family, but also for all humanity."

"I'm not sure what you mean by that Father," said Julie.

"We are only divided as human beings because we sin," he said. "When we are healed by God's grace our union with God also restores the union between us and other people. When you receive the sacrament of chrismation God is enabling you to be restored to His likeness. It will not happen immediately, but the sacraments are an important part of that process of restoration. Our whole being exists in a state of division. We are divided within ourselves, and we see this manifested in misery and mental illness and our choosing to sin. But we are also separated from God and from each other, and as God restores us to perfection the divisions are removed."

"This makes sense to me Father, but I'm still not sure what you mean by being divided within ourselves." Julie's spoke with a deep seriousness.

"We have become individualistic, our ego dominates us. This focus on the self is unnatural and destructive. Christ became man to overcome these divisions, to unite us once again with God and with each other. In Christ we see the setting aside of self, the humility of God that is obedient and willing to sacrifice all for the sake of others. When we set ourselves at the centre of our vision of the world we become blind. The man of love exists in unity with all people; he is a universal being rather than an individualistic one. Therefore your chrismation is an important moment in your personal journey, your own salvation, but it has a wider impact too. We must see ourselves as not only belonging to the whole human race but doing everything as though we were representing them. When I sin it is as though the whole human race sins, and when I love then all men are blessed. When Christ was resurrected it was a reality for all humanity. The shackles of death were broken for all of us, and we must continue to love in order to redeem not just ourselves but the humanity we share in."

Julie nodded at his words, "So we must repent not just for ourselves but for all people, even our children."

"Yes, of course," said Father Basil, "we are familiar with the idea that sin is both personal to us but also affects the whole of creation. The same is true of love, repentance, forgiveness. When we are purified and return to God we do so as a part of the whole human race because God does not see us as divided. God looks upon us as we really are, as He created us, united, one to another. We are called to abandon the old man of sin and allow the new man to be born in us."

"But beyond repentance and the sacraments," said Julie, "I'm still not clear what this means."

"It is the denial of self even to the point of crucifixion." Father Basil spoke slowly, "We must mortify the flesh, overcome the individualistic self, so as to be like Christ. Christ did not only take on to Himself our sin but our whole humanity. We are to identify with one another even as we sin. We must be unified in our shared humanity so that we do not judge or reject one another, but love even as the other sins. This is the meaning of the cross; it is God uniting Himself with us in our sin. Each of us must see Christ's death as being for our particular sin, our own personal acts of disobedience. But we must also try to carry the burden of one another's sin. This is the universal nature of our being, and this is what happens when we are truly united with God Who showed us how to love in this way. This is why we say in the Jesus Prayer "Have mercy on me". It is not an individualistic, private plea for mercy, but the prayer offered in recognition that we speak on behalf of all people. We are called to stand beside every sinner, knowing that we are sinners ourselves, and when someone sins against us we do not allow our private hurt to destroy our solidarity with them. Christ prayed for our forgiveness as we hung Him on a cross, how little in comparison we endure for one another."

As his words ended the only sound in the room was the deep breathing of James in my arms. Julie's voice broke the silence: "But we see in our culture a strong emphasis on the freedom of the individual. Do you think this is a bad thing?"

"Of course certain human rights are necessary in a world where there are governments who wish to prevent us from pursuing what we believe to be right. The devil is certainly attacking the right to religious freedom in many parts of the world and time and again we see that it is Christians who suffer most. But there is a terrible danger with the world's promotion of individualism. Children are being taught that their fulfilment in life, their purpose and meaning is to be found in gratifying their egos. Most people are encouraged to compete with one another; humanity is being convinced that their neighbour is a threat to the satisfaction of self and our desires. This is evil, it is satanic. It divides us from one another and ultimately from God. The aim of the demons is to keep us from knowing the unity which flows from love. The demons desire to separate us from one another and from God."

At that moment James opened his eyes and Julie reached into her bag for his bottle. He looked around at the unfamiliar surroundings and fixed his gaze on the stranger before him. His eyes met those of Father Basil and for a moment the two of them quietly looked at each other. Without looking away from him Father Basil said "Children are the greatest icons of God it is possible for us to produce."

The three of us smiled as James lifted his bottle and began to drink, all the time looking intently at the bearded monk before him.

"Forgive me Father," said Julie, "I sense the truth of what you're saying, it feels right, but I don't completely understand it." I was surprised at how forthright Julie was being, there was no level of pretence or polite reserve in her questions: it made me realise how inhibited I often allowed myself to become in Father Basil's presence.

"In James, in you, in me, in all of us is the fullness of what it is to be human." Father Basil now focussed his attention back on us. "In Adam was the potential for the whole human race, our humanity doesn't exist like some Platonic form separate to us, it is not outside of us but in each and every human being. Only when we live in this reality and understand the connection between us can we live the true life that God intended. We must live with and for all humanity, and the moment we turn away from others to seek our own selfish ends is when we sin, when we separate ourselves off, when we divide ourselves from others and from our true self."

"Does that mean the division between us is only an illusion?" I asked.

"No, it is real, just as the potential for union within us is real. The fragmentation of each human individual within himself is also the division of all humanity. When we look at the state of the world, the chaos of war, the alienation of one man from another, it is really the manifestation of the inner division, the fragmentation of the human heart. This is why our task is so vital. We seek God's grace to establish peace in the world by first establishing it within our selves, within our hearts. The Church Fathers often taught about bringing the mind and heart together, this is the internal unity we are talking about. When the mind rests in the heart and the two are unified in prayer, then humanity itself is being healed. The spiritual life is never selfish, though there are modern voices which criticise it for its lack of apparent outward action. Prayer is an act performed for all people, whether the one praying is consciously aware of this or not."

He stood up, and without saying anything offered his open hands to James. I lifted him forwards and Father Basil confidently lifted him from me. James continued to drink but glanced quickly at his mother for confirmation that all was well. Father Basil smiled at the child in his arms who was now reaching out and burying his hand into his beard.

"This small person is a mirror of the image and likeness of God. Sadly we cover much of the surface with the rubbish we learn from other sinful people and from our own weaknesses. But if we work to clean it then the image of God can be reflected out into the world. A child is both connected to everything around him but at the same time in a sense is separate from all things. As we grow older we lose the simplicity of childhood. The monastic life is an attempt to regain this balance of connection and separation; we separate ourselves from many things in life so that we can become truly united with all men."

He handed James back to me, "Would you like to see the icon studio?"

"Yes, very much," said Julie.

Father Basil led us up a narrow stairway to the room directly above where we had been sitting. It had a large window through which natural light flooded the space. There were jars and pots on a number of shelves and in the middle of the room three icons in various stages of completion sat on home-made stands. Two were of the Theotokos, the third of a woman saint that I did not recognise. The room conveyed a sense of activity but also good order. Everything had its place and every surface was clean and cared for.

"They're stunning," said Julie, "are they all your work?"

"Yes," said Father Basil, "But they are inferior to the icon you have created."

He gave us a brief explanation of the painting process and showed us different paints that he described mixing for different effects. James was transfixed by it all; the colours had a vivid intensity that was nothing like anything he had seen before.

"I remember you explaining about the patterns you follow," said Julie, "but I can see you definitely have your own style."

"The iconographer does not slavishly copy other icons, but there are accepted forms that are used in order that the saint may be recognised," he explained.

"But why do some iconographers become so famous then?" I asked. "I can understand why Picasso or Van Gogh should be remembered, but if you are following traditions so closely, why are certain iconographers singled out?"

"Of course the work of some people is particularly striking for its beauty, but it is more than that." He paused for a moment and then continued. "All artists put something of them self in their work. The secular artist may express their emotions, or their work may capture their imagination or their intellectual ideas. And these can be edifying when the thing being expressed is noble or of value. But something far more important of the iconographer is put into his work: the icon reflects his faith. When we look at an icon we see the faith of the artist shining through, and just as a political artist tries to stir up sympathies for their ideas through their work, icons invite us to respond in faith. But something else is happening with the icon that is beyond what the viewer brings to it. When we engage with the spiritual reality portrayed in an icon we can experience God's grace. It is grace which grants us faith, and God reaches out to us through the icon painted in faith. In this way the unity we were speaking of earlier is manifest when we stand before the icon because our physical senses work to serve the heart. We come to the icon as whole people and encounter God in our whole person."

The icons around us, even half-finished, began to take on an added dimension of significance and I could sense the faith he himself had put into his work.

Father Basil continued, "We talked about being icons of God, we could say that just as we see the iconographer's faith in the painting, then the world around us should see our faith when they look at our lives."

This point struck me with great force and I knew only too well how many other things were manifest in my life other than faith. James was beginning to get restless and Father Basil suggested that we take him out into the fresh air. We made our way into the sunshine and James quickly realised that no one was going to stop him exploring the open space in front of the house. He tottered off to the nearest tree and made himself busy exploring the stones scattered around at its base. There was a bench to the side of the building and the three of us sat facing the sun, watching James at play. He asked us about our experience of parish life and Julie expressed her continuing concern over living so far from the rest of the community.

"I understand your feelings," said Father Basil, "but we must try to accept where we are at any moment without thinking that this is the way it will always be. Very often even trials that seem insurmountable turn out to be ways that God is leading us to greater blessings."

"It's not just the isolation from everyone," added Julie, "the sheer distance is exhausting."

I was uncomfortable with this statement; I wanted to hide these concerns in order not to appear resentful. Julie however was continuing to speak openly and honestly.

Father Basil nodded his understanding, "There is a story about a monk living in the Egyptian desert who had to walk many miles each day to fetch water for his elder. When asked why he did this he said he did so out of obedience knowing that God counted every step he took as being in his favour. Be assured that every mile you drive is seen by God, He knows when we are putting in the effort required of us, it will not go unrewarded. Try to accept that this is the way it is for now and trust that all is in God's hands."

"We are very grateful for Father Philotheos, he has given us a lot if his time," I added.

"He is a good parish priest," said Father Basil, "I am sure you are in good hands. He has had a lot of ill health in recent years, but seems to be recovering now."

We were surprised at this news but didn't enquire any further. James had found his way back to us and his arrival prompted Father Basil to invite us to take a look at the finished guest house. "The monastery is growing in so many ways," he said, "the bricks and mortar are a sign of God's blessing." The work had clearly been finished some time ago and the whole structure had been weathered enough to look more like the rest of the buildings. Eventually we found our way back to the kitchen table for a final coffee. To my horror I discovered that Julie had left the tea she had specifically asked for and while Father Basil was out of the room I pulled a disapproving look at her. Again she dismissed my reaction which only frustrated me further.

When he came back he asked "Have you found anything at all about Orthodoxy that is giving you concern?"

We thought for a moment and then both assured him that there was nothing. "Good," he said, "there are some people who find the differences between their previous traditions and those of Orthodoxy a difficult obstacle to climb."

"We were a little surprised when Father Philotheos told us at first to remain Anglican if we could," I said.

Father Basil smiled, "Yes, that is good advice. If someone is able to remain where they are then they are not ready for Orthodoxy. The Church isn't out knocking on doors trying to convert new members; God's Kingdom is for those who truly want it."

The morning had passed quickly and with James in mind we wanted to head back while there was still plenty of daylight. Father Basil invited us to visit the chapel before we left in order to venerate the icons. At the iconostasis he took James in his arms and lifted him to each of the saints in turn, carefully bringing his face up to each icon. It moved us to see this and as I watched I knew I was being taught what to do when I was next in church. Finally he stood before the icon of the Theotokos and read a prayer from one of the books on the stand. We bowed our heads as he prayed, aware of her presence with us and confident that she would join us in our prayers to her Son. The familiar smell of the beeswax candles had become a constant accompaniment to prayer and never failed to evoke a sense of mystery to me, a sweetness that was pointing to something beyond our selves. Father Basil prayed without any expression of emotion but as he spoke the words I sensed that every one of them was coming from his heart.

Outside he walked with us to the gate where he gave James a small laminated icon of Saint James the Apostle.

"Keep in touch, and we shall pray for your reception." He stroked James' head, "take confidence that God's hand is over you. Pray for one another, and for the monastery."

We thanked him for his time and departed with great joy. As we walked along the lane to the car Julie said "Thank you for bringing me. I see why you keep coming."

"Why on earth did you ask for tea and then not drink it?"

"I forgot he wouldn't have milk in Lent, I couldn't drink it black." She was amused at my question.

I shook my head; even knowing I was being silly didn't stop me being annoyed.

"Are you worried about what he'll think of you?" She asked. It was true, but I couldn't admit it.

"No," I insisted, "it just felt rude." I was beginning to feel foolish.

"Oh really," she continued to smile to herself, "I think you're a bit desperate for his approval."

I didn't want to hear it and despite the effect the monastery had had on me, I had to work hard to conceal my feelings. As I buckled James into position once more Julie came round behind me. As I straightened up she slipped her arms around me and held me tight.

"I love you," she whispered, lifting every trace of annoyance from me. I held her tight and secretly thanked God for her.

As we drove home we talked about what Father Basil had said and shared our different reflections. It was then that Julie said something that brought back an experience from an earlier visit.

"When we were in the chapel," she said, "I thought I saw someone standing beside Father Basil."

"When?"

"As he was praying for us, just out of the corner of my eye, I thought someone was next to him. When I looked there was no one, but just for a moment I could have sworn..." her voice trailed off. I didn't say anything about the impression the frescoes had made on me, I knew Julie was strongly opposed to trusting in anything like that, but I sensed it was more than a trick of the light.

A few weeks later we were standing in church as Father Philotheos read prayers over us. A few of the congregation had turned out to support us with their prayers and friendship but this time none of our family were present to see James baptised. As we were anointed with oil and finally welcomed into the Body of the Church I felt enormous relief and gratitude. The following morning at the Liturgy on Palm Sunday our sponsors accompanied us to the iconostasis to receive Holy Communion for the first time. I wasn't sure what to expect after so much time and preparation, and there was certainly no immediate spiritual elation that came over us. But as we stood amongst the other members of the congregation a powerful peace filled my heart and mind. For the first time ever I knew with absolute certainty that we had truly received Christ's Body and Blood, that we had obeyed His commandment and that we could have complete confidence in knowing that we were part of the Church. The absence of doubt wasn't something I had ever known before and as I looked at James holding his mother's hand I understood how God had been leading us through the past ten years. But despite the sense of relief I understood that this was the beginning of a new part of our journey, not the conclusion of the story. We had travelled to the foot of the mountain and only now were we about to begin the climb: this was our entry into the battle that had begun at Pentecost.

1986

Visits to the monastery became an important part of our life. The usual struggles of maintaining a family were somehow easier to bear after speaking to Father Basil and most importantly time spent with him always rejuvenated our desire for God. The long drives to church didn't seem so long, our relative lack of money didn't appear as important and our sense of purpose and meaning while conducting the trivial activities of the day were always magnified. The simplicity of his life and the pure focus of his existence gave clarity to everything and for a while at least after seeing him we were not quite so petty or angry or subject to any of the other human failings that afflict our lives: but of course sustaining this was a different matter.

The approach of Pascha reminded us of the previous year's events and we agreed that it had been too long since we had last spoken to Father Basil. I made the arrangements and a few weeks later we found ourselves once more sitting at the table where he entertained guests. As he tended to the task of hospitality and brewed the tea, I felt a sense of satisfaction that Julie and James were now sitting here as members of the Orthodox Church. Amidst the mistakes and foolishness of my life I at least knew I had done one thing right and now being in the monastery I sensed a different connection between our lives and that of the monks. It had never occurred to me before but the boundaries between family and monastic life now seemed erased and I had a clear understanding of how we were each a part of the One Body, the One Church. The monks' lives were very different to ours, but at the heart of their calling was the same impulse to seek God that every human being is blessed with (though some of us manage to bury it deep enough to be able to ignore it).

Father Basil joined us and as he began pouring the drinks asked "How are you finding being Orthodox?"

I wasn't sure how to reply but Julie had no hesitations "It's been a real relief," she said, "the parish has made us very welcome. It's good to belong to a worshipping community again."

"And it's good to be getting somewhere spiritually," I added. Father Basil gave me a quizzical look and I regretted my attempt at sounding serious.

"Don't disregard your life before becoming Orthodox," he said. "Try to see the whole of your life as a single continuous struggle. Of course there is a difference now that you are part of the Church, but you mustn't discount what God was doing for you to get you to this point." He stirred the tea and handed out the cups. Julie had introduced James to tea as soon as he was old enough and he now looked quite comical sitting with a large monastery cup, barely able to see over the edge of the table.

"Our spiritual development begins with the natural knowledge that God gives to every man Stewart. This may come to us through the scriptures, or through other people or the angels sent to help us when we are chrismated. All three of you are now assisted by angelic powers."

"I believe this Father," said Julie, "but what does it mean? How do they help us?"

"Your Guardian Angel prays with and for you. You must get into the habit of being aware of the angel that prays with you. He works to protect you; God has not let you wander onto the battle field alone."

"How does our angel protect us Father?" I asked.

"Our Guardian Angel speaks to us through the prompting of our conscience, the more we listen to this inner voice the stronger it becomes. When we are tempted to sin and we respond to our conscience it becomes more powerful and we are winning the fight. But our angel also reminds us of Christ's commandments, and if we are obedient to these then we preserve the grace that we receive at our baptism."

"You make it sound so easy Father," Julie smiled as she spoke, "when I look at how I live I see only struggle with sin."

"That is good," he said. "This is the true nature of the Christian life. I do not believe that any of us make spiritual progress when life is perfectly peaceful; we need these times of struggle in order that we can be strengthened. Of course God grants us time of peace because we are weak. And alongside God's grace is our own capacity to make choices. Obedience is the abandonment of our own will to the will of God. Salvation is found in obedience. The monk doesn't flee only attachment to the things of this world, more importantly he flees from his own will. This is the voluntary death we find in caves, in forests, in the quiet rooms of monasteries. Hope in God's promises frees us from attachment and this leads us to love of God. Self love is really no more than the love of one's own will and when we give up on it we are protected from everything that the devil or the world can throw at us because we are slaves to God, and this is the road that leads to becoming gods by grace. It doesn't matter if we are married or living as monks, obedience to God is the same for all people in all ages. And there have been men and women who have perished or been saved in every form of life and in every age. The outward differences have no bearing on the spiritual reality of our lives."

"Obedience is difficult," I admitted.

"Yes, and we must understand what it is we are referring to. Even wild beasts can be trained to be obedient, but they gain no eternal reward for this. We who are far greater than wild animals so often reduce ourselves to being beneath them. The sheep and cattle happily share the land of pasture, each animal happily grazing without jealousy, but man desires more than he can ever use or need. We who have been given dominion over the animals bring ourselves lower than them through our passions. We are confused by the pleasures of the world, our laziness and selfish inclinations pull us in the wrong direction. Saint Ilias said that just as the rays of the physical sun cannot penetrate a shuttered house neither can the light of God illuminate the soul that has its senses fixed on visible or material things. As a husband and wife you must deal with the demands of organising your family life, and this is very important, but devotion to God is not a distraction or alternative to this, it is the way that you succeed in doing it properly." He looked at James who was sitting quietly listening to the conversation around him. "You have a responsibility to nurture the life and faith of your son, and God will call you to account for the responsibility he has entrusted you with. But the world is working against you in this. You may be the last generation of westerners to grow up untainted by the bombardment of television. The soul is deformed, disfigured by the stream of images and ideas that the television is allowed to pour into young children. Western civilisation will reap a terrible reward for what it is doing to its children. So many of them are growing up without any connection to the created world. They are out of touch with the land or the seasons, their sense of community and belonging has been severed. Instead they are handed over to the electronic machine that jumbles their minds and fills them with satanic influences. I truly believe that the television is one of the greatest destructive forces in our world today. Take enormous care how you allow it to impinge on your lives, and especially that of your child."

"We have a television Father," I said, "do you think we should get rid of it?"

"That is a question you must answer for yourselves. Consider how much of your time it occupies and how much of an influence it has over you. But your focus must be to allow beauty and holiness to blossom in your son's life: if you perceive television to be working against this then yes, get rid of it. A time will come when more technology will appear; I believe that television is only the first step. Watching television has already become the normal way that many families spend their evenings, but this is only the first stage. It is a kind of conditioning to prepare people for what is next."

"Where do you think it is leading?" I asked.

"Satan's desire is to isolate people, separate us from our friends, families and neighbours. I see in this technology a way for people to feel that they are connected with others without any real connection existing at all. Flashing pictures of people will come to replace direct human contact. Western people are being made numb to their lack of human relationship. And if we do not know what relationship is then we cannot know God. Real existence is being exchanged for fantasies, the mind itself is being trained to think and see the world in an artificial way. The makers of television programmes are not sympathetic to the souls of their viewers; their goal is to make money. Programmes exist only to make money. And so there will be a steady slide away from everything that is noble and dignified towards the sordid and sensational: in a few years human beings portrayed on television will be unrecognisable as anything that people from the past would understand or know to be human. It is hard for us to imagine what it will be like because we grew up in a different world, but soon the generations before television will be gone and there will be no link back to that other world."

"Forgive me Father," said Julie, "but how do you maintain that human relationship when you live as a monk?"

"The monastic life is not a withdrawal from human relationships. Instead of a single spouse or a particular family, the monk abandons these specific relationships so that he may enter a deeper relationship with all people." He smiled to himself, "There are also plenty of opportunities to learn patience and forgiveness when we live closely in a monastic community. I have known monks who have had to struggle with all kinds of difficulties in their relationships, sometimes at a very profound level; the monastic life requires us to become more human not less." He continued to smile as he recalled what this meant to him and we were left in no doubt that there was a history of very real human relationships behind his words.

"Father," said Julie, "how did you become a monk? What made you decide to follow this way of life?"

"The call to monasticism is not something easily explained; certainly monasticism itself is a supernatural phenomenon that is beyond the expression of language. Monasticism in one sense is beyond the natural understanding of the world; it can only be understood through experience."

"But when did you first decide God wanted you to pursue this life?" Julie persisted.

"At a very young age I felt overwhelmed with the realisation that God wanted me to live this way, and this again, is something not easily explained. Monasticism is a mystery, and the way God leads each person to it is specific to them. Many people test out what they believe God is saying to them, some spend many years living this way before finally realising that raising a family is God's will for them. But I had no such uncertainty; I understood that my life was to follow this path even when I was a teenager. This may sound difficult for some people in the world to accept, those who consider themselves wise in the theories of psychology may protest at someone making a commitment like this at such an early age. But I had no difficulties knowing what God wanted of me, for which I am very grateful."

"I remember you told me about your background in Romania," I was keen to understand how he could have come to such a conclusion so young, "did your parents have an influence on you?"

"Of course," he said, "every parent exerts a great influence on their child whether for good or evil. You know this yourself when you look at James here and how you are bringing him up to love the Church. I too was blessed with parents who loved God and helped me to know Him."

He smiled warmly, a gesture that was as much prompted by memories of his parents as by us sitting before him.

"Please Father, would you tell us about your life?" Julie's question was delivered with enough sincerity to convey her genuine motive for asking.

"As you said, I was born in Romania, in a small village to the North. It was just after the war and people were still suffering the consequences of that terrible conflict. Many families lived without fathers who never returned from the fighting and their burdens were great. My father was a shepherd who had very little education. But he could read and while he was out in the fields he would often take writings from the Fathers with him. Our priest would lend him books which he had an incredible ability to recall even after only one reading. He would often help the widows of the village by doing jobs on their houses and so on; his heart was full of compassion for everyone around him. This part of the Balkans was a blessed part of the world.

Village and Church life were one, holy days were celebrated by the whole community and the beauty of nature was all around us. It was common to find everyone celebrating feast days together, all work would come to an end when the church bells rang. My earliest memories are of my father sitting on the hillside reading extracts from the Church Fathers aloud. I would pretend to play nearby but all the time I listened to his voice and through his lips heard the wisdom of God. I watched him closely, how he would enter church, how he always carried himself with great humility and simplicity. He was very strict at times but whenever I was punished I always knew it pained him to have to discipline me, such was his love for me."

He paused for a moment, and without any sentimentality crossed himself. "My mother too was a good woman who worked hard for her family. I had three brothers and my mother was always busy providing us with meals or clean clothes to wear. My youngest brother died when we were young and I remember his funeral very well. My mother's heart was broken but through her grief shone her faith and trust in God. I remember one night when she caught me weeping for my little brother, she told me to ask him to pray for us, which I did often from that day. My grief was softened and I understood a little more about the reality of life and death.

There was a priest in the village who we would see all the time. Nothing was done by anyone without first asking him to bless the endeavour. He would always have time for our questions and when my father died early he would ensure that my mother had bread for her sons. Being widowed left my mother with great financial hardship, and though we knew she had many difficulties, we never heard her complain. She taught us so much through her example and even though we were only teenagers when we lost our father she did not allow us to fall into self-pity. I do not recall a single day after his death when she did not pray for him; such was her love and faith.

I remember the icon corner in our house always had a lamp burning, and there were times when we would find our mother praying in the night after having worked long hours at her job. She would kneel before the icon of the Mother of God holding us before God in her prayers. One time my eldest brother left home without explanation and after a week of worry my mother discovered he was living in a near-by large town leading a sinful life. She took a train ride and found him, and I was overjoyed when she returned with him. He never told me what she'd said to persuade him to come home, but of the two of us he remained the more obedient son until she died."

"What was life like under the Communists?" I asked.

Father Basil nodded in his thoughtful manner, "It was hard for many people. The Communists were brutal, they attacked the Church with great ferocity and many clergy and ordinary people suffered at their hands. Our own priest was threatened but refused to stop preaching his sermons. The Communists took him away and no one ever found out what happened to him. One of his sons tried to raise his case but could find no answers. He too was threatened and was forced to drop his enquiries. The pain of this was felt for many years and even to this day there are people living amongst their neighbours who still have a hand in the persecutions. Somehow retribution has been avoided; it is the mark of a good people that they can forgive such things, but while the Church is oppressed evil is free to stalk the land.

We always attended church services and even under the watchful eyes of the state we continued to live out our faith. The new priest came from many miles away and had no real understanding of village life. He did what he could but we knew he was fearful of what might happen to him and so services were cut short and he was careful to avoid saying anything that might land him in trouble. Watching this I felt great pity for him, it was no surprise when his nerves eventually crumbled and he became too sick to even sing the Liturgy.

About eight miles from our village there was a monastery dedicated to Saint Anthony of the Desert. Once a year my brother and I would walk to make our confession and receive spiritual counsel. There was a monk there, Father Ambrose, who was an incredible man, word of his prayerfulness spread wide and far. The Communists left him alone because they were afraid of how people would react if anything happened to him, such was his reputation. The very first time I visited I was struck by the peace in his face and when he heard my confession it was as though a great weight had been lifted from my shoulders. His advice spoke to my heart, and the presence of God filled the air in that place. Even within the atmosphere of hostility created by the Communists, I saw the things of this world as they truly are and knew I wanted nothing but God: something I realised could only be satisfied for me through monasticism. The example of Father Ambrose taught me that the spiritual life is where we learn about death and immortality, this is really the heart of all spirituality. I knew I must become a monk. I first mentioned this to my brother as we walked home from one of our visits and he immediately confirmed that this was his intention also. He remained in Romania and is now abbot of a community about eighty miles from our village.

A few years passed this way and with the passing of time my longing to become a monk grew. But I knew that my mother was struggling and I felt a compulsion to take care of her. I had not spoken to her about my longings and began to believe that they could never be satisfied. God however, saw to it that I would become a monk. When I had turned sixteen I left school to seek work at a factory just an hour's bus ride away. The chemicals that we were exposed to in this work had a bad effect on my health and I began to suffer head aches and vomiting. I tried to hide this from my mother but eventually I became so sick that I went into a state of delirium. The doctor could do nothing for me and as my fever increased it looked as though my poor mother would suffer the loss of another son. She spent long hours in vigil for me, praying ceaselessly and weeping tears of intercession. On the third night she was pleading with the Mother of God to intercede for me when she heard a gentle voice calmly reassuring her. The woman's voice told her to anoint me with oil from the icon of the Theotokos that was in church and that all would be well. She dashed through the dark in the middle of the night but found the church locked. Not concerning herself with appearance she went to the home of the priest and demanded entry to the church. Thankfully the priest let her in and she took some of the oil that she needed. The priest accompanied her to my bedside and helped her to anoint me in my sickness. They continued to pray together, both filled with the conviction of faith that what had been promised would come true. By morning my temperature had fallen and by lunch time I was sitting up and able to speak. My mother had no doubts that we had been granted a miracle which made it easier for me to raise the possibility of entering a monastery. Without any hesitation or thought for herself she gave me her blessing. My brother too received the news with joy and I understood my illness as God's means of gaining me release from the claims of the world.

A few months later I had arranged to visit Saint Anthony's with the hope of entering the monastic life. There was no major feast that day and so there were few pilgrims around. Father Ambrose received me in his cell and we prayed together before his icons. We sat near his fire, my heart brimming with the excitement of revealing my intentions. But my hopes were dashed when he began to tell me a story about a young man who had entered a monastery against his elder's wishes and who had suffered in all kinds of ways for many years as a result. As he told the story I sensed only too clearly that it was his way of breaking bad news to me. I hadn't revealed my plans to him and yet he was able to perceive them without being told. After his story ended he looked at me with great attention and told me that he did not believe God wanted me to be part of the community there. Even knowing that this was coming my heart sank when he said it and I was barely able to hold back my tears. He comforted me with a sweet biscuit and told me not to doubt that all things were in God's hands. I managed to ask him whether this meant I should not become a monk at all and the only reassurance he would give was that he wasn't saying this, only that Saint Anthony's was not to be my home. I remained there for a few days and though still very disappointed, I returned home trying to be patient in waiting for God to show me what was next. In the meantime I found a different job which was healthier and closer and the next six months passed quite comfortably. It was then that we heard that the Communists has closed Saint Anthony's monastery and the whole community had been arrested. Despite people's anger there were no marches in protest, no rallies or campaigns, the monks simply became more names added to the list of the disappeared. My frustration at not getting my own way now looked very different and I thanked God for not giving in to my demands.

It was another three years before I was able to fulfil my dream of monasticism. My brother told me that he was happy to take care of our mother. In fact mother only lived for two more years, but released from my responsibilities I was at last able to approach another monastery. I stayed there for less than eighteen months, the Communists were too involved in the community's activities and it was too affected by the world to make progress in prayer possible. The abbot had the opportunity of sending one of his community to Mount Athos in Greece and thanks be to God he chose me. It was there that I was tonsured and given the name Basil. But God's will was not that I should stay on the Holy Mountain, within two years I came to England, but it meant I was free to travel in a way that would never have been possible if I had stayed in Romania."

We had listened in complete silence, even James had been captivated by the sound of Father Basil's voice. It had come as a surprise to hear him share in such intimate detail the events of his life. We knew that it was a great act of trust to reveal so much of him self and in allowing us to know him in such a way.

"Thank you for sharing with us Father," said Julie, "I never could have imagined that your life would be so different from what we know in this part of the world."

"Sadly the persecution of God's people continues through out the Soviet Block. Bishops, priests and especially monks are threatened, beaten and even killed. But the western churches know nothing of this because to speak out is to put so many of our loved ones at risk." His eyes filled with tears, "To be Christian under Communism is to accept that cruelty or death may come at any time. Many holy men and women have become martyrs under this yoke; we are living in the age of Christian martyrs. But it will not continue for ever. Many saints have foreseen the end of this regime, Russia and Romania will blossom once more. We must pray and continue to wait on God."

James was becoming a little restless and so Father Basil suggested that we take a stroll around the newly planted trees that he was taking care of. "One day this will be a woodland of native trees," he said, "it reminds us that we must not be so impatient as to want everything now. We invest our effort and who knows if we will be around to witness the results, but our enjoyment is secondary, the fact is they will grow. We do not always get to see the harvest of the seeds we have sown. But we are working for God, not our selves; we should learn to be happy in serving Him."

We asked a little more about Romania and he told us about the monasteries in various parts of the country. Eventually we found our way back to the monastery buildings and it seemed a natural time to depart.

"Thank you for letting us come," said Julie, "we cannot thank you enough for your time."

"Thank you for coming," said Father Basil, "it is always good to meet people who thirst for God."

We exchanged farewells and were soon back in the car heading for home. As we drove we talked about Father Basil's life and how fortunate we were to be practising our faith so freely. It was a freedom I had never been aware of, something I had simply taken for granted, but as we drove I began to contemplate the millions of Christians enduring the reality of Communist atheism. I sensed the dark forces that exist in the world and the terrible evils that men mistake for answers to their pain. I knew that the trivial concerns of our lives were often an illusion, a fake reality in which we happily wasted the precious years given to us by God.

1987

I found myself driving alone to the monastery while Julie stayed at home to nurse James through a cold. It was a warm summer morning and as I always did I was enjoying the sunshine in my face as I drove. About two miles from the monastery I spotted a man hitch-hiking at the side of the road and prompted by thoughts of Christian compassion and thoughts of where I was headed I slowed down as I approached him.

I leaned over the passenger seat to wind down the window, "Where are you headed?" I shouted.

The man jogged over to the side of the car and as he drew near I could see his clothes were stained from a life of travelling. I immediately regretted the decision to stop but knew that it was too late to withdraw the offer. "I'm going to the monastery," he said, leaning too fully into the open window.

"Jump in, that's where I'm going." As he dropped into the seat I discreetly assessed the condition of his clothes and wondered how my upholstery was going to look after he got out.

"Thank you very much," his breath was sweet with sherry and as he turned to speak to me I had to consciously overcome the urge to pull my head away. The car was quickly filled with the smell of dried, stale sweat and my fantasies about how the visit would go were quickly crumbling.

"You seein' Father Basil?" He asked.

"Yes," I said, "what about you?"

"Oh yea, I always pop in on him when I'm round these parts. He's like a brother to me. Always makes me feel welcome. My name's John." I took the hand he extended towards me and introduced my self. "You been to the monastery before?" He continued.

"Yes, I've been coming for a few years now," I didn't want to mention Julie, for some inexplicable reason it seemed risky to even say her name here in the car with him. But as my suspicion was running wild his next statement disarmed my paranoia and I relaxed.

"He's a very holy man, God is in his heart," he said.

"I agree," I said, relieved to hear him express the sentiment, "we're lucky to be able to come out and see him."

"Luck ain't got nothin' to do with it Stewart, it's God's will. God put him on this earth to help people like you and me, ain't no luck in it at all."

I agreed with him and regretted saying it; it was a thoughtless comment that didn't really express how I felt. "No, you're right," I said.

Ten minutes later I let John get out and pulled in tight against the hedge in the usual parking space. He stood in the middle of the road, watching my manoeuvre with great attention and I kept expecting him to start calling out instructions. We walked the last section of lanes side by side, my frustration growing as his continuous chatter interrupted my plan to arrive focussed and in what I considered to be a suitably spiritual state of mind.

At the door of the monastery I knocked a few times but then John pushed passed me and turned the handle. He forced open the door and poking his head through the gap called out "Hello, anyone home?" I was embarrassed by his behaviour and wanted to somehow separate myself from him but there was nowhere to run. As John stepped in to the building I hesitated outside, unsure how to react to his boldness. The monastery was a strange mixture of public space and private home, and I could no more feel comfortable walking in uninvited as I could into my neighbour's house.

I then heard another man's voice and a brief muffled conversation began. The bearded face of a young monk who I didn't recognise suddenly appeared at the door.

"Come in," he instructed, "I will let Father Basil know you have arrived." John was already sitting at the table, "You putting the kettle on Father?" He shouted playfully. The young monk didn't answer but headed into the kitchen to prepare our tea. "Sit down Stewart," John continued to act very much at home and I began to wonder if he was a more frequent visitor than I had realised. I slid in on the bench beside him, my discomfort continuing to rise. He began recounting details of his previous visits in a voice that was unnecessarily loud and so I compensated by responding in a voice that was barely audible.

The monk returned carrying a tray and as he lay it down and began to pour our drinks he introduced himself as Father Seraphim. It was a relief to have someone else to talk to, and I made an effort to direct conversation towards him.

"How long have you been at the monastery Father?"

"Nearly six months," he said, "I was in Essex before this."

"I've visited the monks down there," announced John, "great fellas, always make me welcome they do."

Father Seraphim went off to look for Father Basil and for a moment at least John fell silent as he sipped at his tea. "No biscuits," he muttered, "it ain't Lent."

Eventually the door opened and Father Basil appeared, his beard longer and whiter than ever before, but he carried the same reassuring smile I had hoped to see again.

"Hello Stewart, welcome, it is good to see you." He kissed my cheeks and my mood improved. John was trapped behind the table but the two men exchanged friendly greetings. Father Basil lifted the top off the tea pot and discovering it was still half full poured him self a cup.

"John has spent years exploring Britain, I think he must know the roads better than anyone."

"That I do Father, but it don't come easy. I'm getting too old for it now; I need a place to settle down more permanent."

"Have you approached the council about a flat? Last time you were here that was your plan John."

"No Father, I ain't got round to it yet. There's always other things I have to take care of.." He paused a little sheepishly and then asked "I was wondering if there might be a chance of stayin' here for a few days."

"I'm sorry John, but we have a group arriving this evening, I told you before about ringing before turning up like this." There was a stern tone to Father Basil's voice that I hadn't heard before and I could sense his annoyance.

"I won't cause 'em any trouble Father, how about just the one night?"

"I'm sorry John, that isn't going to be possible." John looked genuinely disappointed at the news and for a moment no one said anything. But then choosing a different approach John said "I really need some cash Father, I've run up a couple of debts. Any chance you could let us 'ave a few quid? I could pay you back when I'm next up this way."

"No!" Father Basil's voice was just short of a shout but it made me jump. "I'm not going down this path again. We will feed you and give you what we can, but no money this time."

"I need to talk to you Father," he glanced across at me, "sorry Stewart, don't mean to be rude." I wasn't sure if he was asking me to leave the room and I looked to Father Basil for some indication of what I should do. But before I could figure it out

John asked "Can we go into the chapel for a little while?"

"Yes," said Father Basil, "please Stewart, help your self to tea and have a look at the books over there." I stood to allow John out from behind the table and the two of them left to deal with whatever it was John had on his mind. The sudden silence in the room made me aware of myself and what I was thinking and I realised how selfishly I had been secretly reacting the whole time. I couldn't find any real concern in my heart for John at that moment, only frustration and resentment. I was ashamed to see this in myself but recognising it was easier than correcting it. I began looking through the book shelf and found a photographic journal about Mount Athos. The text was in Greek but I was content to look at the pictures in which the shining faces of various monks looked out from a world I could barely imagine. The holiness of the men was mysteriously apparent even in photographs, and I began to compare my reactions to John to how I imagined they might react in this situation. The spiritual thoughts I had played with on my journey had quickly vanished when faced with the demands of a difficult human being, but here I could see men who lived out the reality of those aspirations in the tangible dust and heat of real existence. So much of my own desire for God was nothing more than thoughts of one kind or another, and at that moment I could see clearly the gulf between truth and fantasy: it was a painful realisation.

I continued with the book for a while but then became concerned when I heard raised voices outside. I couldn't make out what was being said but one of the voices definitely belonged to Father Basil. This left me a little confused and I moved to the door to try and hear more clearly. I still couldn't make out what was happening and so opened the door to see if there was anything I should do. Before me were the two men, but John had now fallen silent. Father Basil however continued to loudly chastise him.

"Don't ever return to the monastery unless you can behave appropriately," he shouted. "There can be no more mistakes, I will not have this John, do you understand what I am saying?"

John caught sight of me in the doorway and looked ashamed. His eyes were filling with tears and I felt a compulsion to defend him. I stood rooted to the spot, the scene was disorientating, nothing made sense. I couldn't equate this angry man with the Father Basil I thought I knew. Finally the shouting stopped and Father Basil turned to me and said "I will have to drive John into the village; I will be back in about half an hour." With that he turned and headed off behind the church where the monastery van was parked. John hesitated for a moment, it looked as though he were about to try and explain something to me, but then without a word he followed our host like a naughty child. A moment later I watched the van pulling away and was left standing alone, wondering what I should do. The volume of their voices had alerted Father Seraphim who now reappeared and waved me into the house.

We sat down at the table but he didn't offer any explanation about what had happened. I couldn't let it go and asked "Is everything alright with Father Basil?"

Seeing my concern he said "Oh yes, this is nothing new. I understand John has been coming for a few years and has always been welcome. But about two years ago he took some money from another pilgrim who was staying at the time. Father Basil persuaded the man not to press charges against John and offered to refund the money. He didn't take it, and agreed to let that be the end of the matter. When John next came to the monastery Father made it clear to him that he could only come under certain conditions: that he must be sober while at the monastery and that he could not have access to the guest room when other people were staying. He has kept to these rules until now, but we did catch him taking money from the chapel a few months ago. Father has done everything he can to help him, and I am sure we will see John again before long, but he had obviously been drinking. I don't know what John got up to in the church this time, but it must have been something serious for Father Basil to have to speak to him so severely." He smiled at this; it was obvious there was no lingering animosity towards their visitor. "I have a little work I must complete before lunch; will you be alright until Father returns?"

"Yes, of course, thank you, I'll go and sit in the sunshine while I wait."

I had my prayer rope with me and tried to make the most of the time on my hands. But my thoughts kept wondering and the picture of Father Basil kept filling my mind. I had perceived the externals of the situation without any understanding of its reality. And paradoxically I had worked hard to present a polite appearance while secretly harbouring rejection of John. We had been polar opposites in our reactions, and it was sickening to have to acknowledge to myself that I had only been concerned with presenting the right image. My falsehood was a combination of man-pleasing and pride and was a bitter realisation. I sat, a little disheartened, listening for the van to arrive. I was so caught up in my emotions that I couldn't see the stunning day that existed around me.

Eventually the approaching van brought me out of my self and I immediately became aware of the sun's rays on my head. It was like waking up having been dropped there while asleep, suddenly I could hear the bird song and I was aware of the smell of the trees in the breeze. I headed to the back of the building to meet him and as I rounded the corner I stopped dead in my tracks. He was standing beside the van, his arm extended and his fingers cupped. Sitting in his hand was a sparrow. He wasn't feeding it; it had simply landed and was now singing gently to him. I froze and tried to take in what I was seeing, there was no fear of any kind in the little bird, and only when it spotted me did it fly away. Father Basil turned and I could see that his face was almost glowing, not with a physical light, but with glow that was beyond light. I couldn't speak; I stared into his face trying to understand what was happening.

As I looked at him he began to speak softly. "When we truly love God, grace fills us so that animals will love us, but they also honour us, for they recognise in us the face of the One Who created us and them." He smiled and the glow left him as his face returned to how it always looked. "While we sink deeper into the world, while we pursue its pleasures, the world becomes ugly and dark to us. But when we are no longer of this world we can come to know the true joy and peace that God grants us while we are still in this world. Only when we belong to Heaven, when we become citizens of Paradise, do we see the beauty and light of this world."

I didn't speak; I was still trying to take everything in. Father Basil moved towards me and taking my arm led me back out into the sunshine. We sat out on the bench looking out across the fields.

Answering the questions that I was unable to say aloud Father Basil said "There is a warmth of heart that only comes to us when we have achieved a certain purity in our prayer. God gives us an energy that brings peace from all thoughts, it illuminates our hearts with grace that leads to perfection. But becoming perfect is an eternal process, God has no limits and we are called to an eternal growth in our knowledge of Him, a growing knowledge that will never end. Pure prayer can only come through experience; no words can communicate to us the living reality of prayer. As I once said to you, the Fathers say that prayer teaches prayer, the soul's life must be embraced and nurtured through our obedience and humility. We must love everyone, black, white, Jew, Christian or Muslim." He paused for a moment and added "drunk or sober," and chuckled a little. "We can only truly love other people when we recognise in them the image of God, we must see this when we look into the face of every man. Prayer without this kind of love is dead; it is like a beautiful bird that has no wings to fly. It is prayer that turns our hearts into thrones for God where He can dwell and reign as King. Prayer has filled Heaven with countless holy saints; it is the most vital activity in all human life."

I knew only too well that such lofty ideas were beyond me, here I was struggling with the petty impulses of my ego and Father Basil was trying to share a reality I could barely hope to ever know or understand. I wanted to hear of these things, but the situation with John had left me feeling ashamed.

"I'm a long way from any of this Father, what can I do to change?"

"First do the little things. Try not to be angry with people, practise generosity and kindness even when you don't feel that way. The more we treat people with kindness the more it grows as a reality within us. Remember your sins and thank God that he has forgiven you. Think of the blessings you have received and try to be grateful for them. Look for one thing every day that you have to be grateful for – this way you will quickly recognise how much God has given you."

I nodded as he spoke, this simple advice made sense to me and I felt he was giving me something I could make use of.

"But kindness and generosity are only part of the battle," he continued. "The spiritual struggle within your self requires a small degree of aestheticism. Our lives are like a full day, prayer is hidden and represents the night, but fasting is outward and seen like daylight. We need the full day if we are to live in the city where there is no suffering. Just like the wheat that grows for the farmer who cares for his fields, true prayer will grow in the Christian who diligently attends to his heart. We must watch over ourselves and allow the virtues of grace to grow, taking care of the young shoots when they first appear. At first this can be a struggle or even a burden. But after a time it becomes a compulsion, like eating is to the hungry man. We begin to thirst and hunger for God and only find satisfaction in prayer. But it is a satisfaction far beyond any filling of the belly; it is a craving of the spirit for union with Christ."

"How do I even begin to do this Father?"

"You must free the intellect from worldly passions. Through self-denial the intellect rises above the material world, through awareness of death it is able to rise up to where the physical needs of the body are nothing. If we continually allow the body to make claims on us we remain slaves. We must be free of our nature so that in prayer we are no longer even aware of ourselves but only of God. Above all we must have humility in all things. Pride strikes us down and makes fools of us in the battle."

Father Basil turned to look at me and could see I was a little dejected. He said "A proud man is blind to his faults, but a humble person never recognises his own virtues. Both are blinded, the first by an evil ignorance, the second by an ignorance that is pleasing to God. Do not lose heart Stewart; trust that God has already won the victory over sin and death. Our struggle is to accept the great gift He now offers to us and become heirs in His Kingdom."

"If I'm honest Father, I find it hard to forgive and be humble. When someone insults me I brood over it and allow resentment to grow."

"It is true that outwardly a man's soul may appear healthy while secretly it is filled with all kinds of afflictions and sickness. Sometimes a soul can be healed by the reproof of others; if we allow their words and actions to humble us it can be greatly beneficial. So God heals even through the outward circumstances of our lives. But this is often painful and we may foolishly reject such cures and insist on our own proud self-justification. The Fathers remind us that we should see the words and actions of others rather like the intervention of a surgeon. When we are cut we bleed, we feel pain, but the treatment for our pride must be accepted and applied. Rather than becoming angry at a person for speaking harshly to us we should look for the cancer that has been cut away and give thanks for the care which God shows us. Reproof strengthens the soul but be careful because praise can debilitate the soul and spread spiritual disease."

"I think my sickness is even more fundamental Father," At last I found myself speaking without any false sense of humility but with genuine contrition, "I am full of sin."

"This is true of all of us Stewart, I am living a life where God grants me the opportunity to pray and focus on the spiritual life, I am free of the cares of family life, I do not have a wife or children to worry about, and yet still I find opportunities to sin. People come to the monastery and imagine us holy men devoid of human passion, but we are all struggling with our fallen nature Stewart, do not mistake us for saints. The task for us all is to remain watchful, to be alert, to recognise sinful impulses and motives when they first appear before they grow in power over us. So long as we do not chain ourselves to small things we will not become tied to big ones: the greater sins always stand on the shoulders of smaller ones. By making ourselves aware of the smaller sins we guard ourselves all the better against the powerful sins. Do not imagine that anything you do is of no consequence; treat every moment of your life as though it is filled with importance. The battle does not always proceed with great explosions, sometimes there are discreet poisonings that bring down even the greatest of warriors."

His words were a comfort and I felt myself less anxious for hearing them. Just then Father Seraphim came out to announce that lunch was ready. Father Basil ushered me in and I found two other monks already waiting: Father John who I recognised from a previous visit and the other was introduced as Father Luke.. They were both older men, grey haired and with faces that revealed many years of asceticism. We bowed our acknowledgements and Father Seraphim laid out dishes of salad, rice and fruit. Once all was settled the monks sang in Greek while facing the icons beside the table. Crossing themselves everyone took their place and I was invited to sit before the remaining empty plate. As we ate Father John stood reading to us from a collection of lives of various contemporary monks on Mount Athos. Sitting beside them I knew I was an alien body, a worldly presence amongst genuine holiness. But I also felt completely accepted; I knew there was no judgement in their hearts, only the Christian love Father Basil had tried to describe to me. Though they sat without conversation, simply being in their company had a calming effect on me, it gave clarity to my sense of the world and made my desire for God feel natural and normal. The monks ate quickly and in response to some signal I hadn't seen everyone simultaneously got to their feet and sang another set of prayers. The dishes were gathered by Father Seraphim who politely declined when I offered to help with the washing up. The monks then separated to attend to their different tasks and while Father Seraphim remained in the kitchen Father Basil offered me coffee in the sunshine.

As I sat waiting for him I felt a sense of satisfaction, I had been nourished in every way and was left with a need to reflect on what had been said. When he joined me Father Seraphim came out too and the two monks began to discuss the greenhouses. I sipped at my coffee, content just to be there at that moment. But I knew I had been granted a generous portion of their time and soon announced that I would be heading back. Father Seraphim took away the cups and Father Basil walked with me to the monastery entrance.

"Thank you for letting me visit Father, it has been a useful trip, as it always is."

"Good, you know you are always welcome."

With that he gave me a brief hug and in his usual unsentimental manner turned and was gone. I took my time walking back to the car; I was trying to give order to my thoughts so that I could reflect on them further, but also so that I could adequately answer Julie's questions when I got home. I began to think about the way Father Basil's face had appeared when I had seen him with the bird and I knew that I wouldn't be able to find a proper description or explanation. I was already having doubts about what I had seen only a couple of hours after the event. If Julie began to push me on the subject I wasn't sure of my ground, I just couldn't rationalise what it meant. In the end I decided not to mention it, at least not until I was confident I understood it more.

1988

I hadn't wanted to go to work but Julie assured me that she could look after him. James had been running a temperature the previous night and had become very weak by the morning. The telephone rang at my desk and it was immediately a concern to hear Julie's voice.

"Stewart, we need to get James to the hospital. His temperature has shot up and he's hardly aware of where he is." Her voice was fraught and kept breaking with emotion. "Get home as quickly as you can."

I made arrangements with my supervisor and within ten minutes was driving back. James had been a relatively healthy child and I knew it took something serious to hit him so hard. I felt a slight panic and prayed through the journey home, imploring the saints to pray with me.

I let my self in to the house and took the stairs two at a time. Julie was sitting on the floor beside James' bed, holding a wet flannel to his forehead. Her cheeks were stained with tears and she looked up at me with a helplessness I had never seen in her before. James lay limply on top of his bed covers, his eyes were half open but he made no response as I entered.

"I've called the doctor but he says he can't come out until after lunch. He's been like this all morning."

I put my hand on her shoulder and tried to reassure her. I noticed a rash on James' chest and knew this could be a bad sign. "I need to check something," I said and rushed down to the kitchen. I found an empty milk bottle that Julia had washed and went back up to James.

"What are you doing?" Julie asked.

"We need to check that rash," I knelt down beside the bed and carefully rolled the bottle over his chest which looked inflamed. It was a technique I had read about and seeing that the red blotches remained dark and intense as the glass moved over them I knew we had to act quickly. "Get his clothes Julie, we need to get him to the hospital straight away."

She quickly pulled out what he needed from his drawers and together we gently pulled his pyjama top over his head. His arms were like a rag doll, and I was alarmed at the heat being emitted from his body. I slid my hands under him and lifted him out of bed. He stirred a little but only enough to let out a weak groan. "Get a coat to put over him," I said, "he mustn't get a chill outside."

Julie sat in the back of the car with him as we dove to the hospital. "Has he had anything to drink this morning?" I asked over my shoulder.

"Nothing," she said, "he must be completely dehydrated."

The car park was busy and I felt my anger building as we looked for a space. It was an anger aimed at the whole world, at the reality of our circumstances for which I was helpless to provide a solution. Once we were parked we wrapped him in his coat and quickly headed to reception. Recognising our concern and seeing the condition he was in a nurse took us straight to a bed and assured us that a doctor would be there soon. She pulled the curtain around us and in this little enclosed space we felt our whole world falling apart. The doctor came quickly and took James' temperature. He asked Julie some brief questions and then told us we would be placed in a quarantined room.

"It could be meningitis," he said, "we can't be sure at this moment. Our priority is to bring his temperature down and rehydrate him." Julie began to cry, all the time holding James' hand.

I carried him behind the nurse who led us to the ward and to our isolated room. The doctor returned within a few minutes and a needle was inserted into James' arm so that an intravenous drip could be fitted. "This will hydrate him and give him a little energy," he explained, "you also need to keep applying moist towels to his head."

It was good to have something practical that we could do, and Julie busied herself with the task. I stood watching, and the nurse turned to me and said "He's a beautiful boy, don't worry, we'll do everything we can." At this I broke into tears, she touched my arm with a reassuring smile and left us with him. I pulled the chairs across to the bedside and began to talk to James. I told him how better he would soon be feeling, how everything was going to be alright, but the words sounded hollow and I fell silent.

The next eight hours or so brought no change in his condition. The nurse kept checking the drip and changing the bowl of water we were using, but there was little else anyone could do. There were a few encouraging fluctuations in his temperature, but each time it came down it quickly rose again. In the whole time we had been there James hadn't said a word and fear began to chip away at our hope.

"Why don't you ring Father Philotheos," said Julie, "we need some one to pray for us." We had each been praying silently, but I knew she was right. I asked at the nurse's station where the public telephone was and followed their directions down the halls. Father Philotheos was very concerned at our news and assured me of his prayers. It was good to speak to someone who wasn't caught up with our immediate situation, and I felt much calmer as I walked back to James' room.

"I don't think they'll let me have tomorrow off work Julie, I'm sorry."

"It's not your fault, besides, losing your job isn't going to help us now."

"Why don't you go home tonight, get some sleep, and come back in the morning," I suggested. "We can be here in shifts. Anyway, there's not room for both of us."

I could see she didn't want to leave, but it made sense and she reluctantly agreed. She stayed another hour and then I told her to go home and get some rest. She bent over James and kissed his cheek, "He's still so hot," she said, "promise me you'll ring me if there's any kind of change, whatever it is."

I promised and finally overcoming her urge to remain she took the car keys from me and forced herself to leave us. Alone with him I bathed his head and began to pray aloud. I called on Saint James, the Mother of God, and every saint that I could recall. Tears streamed down my face once more and I began to recite the Jesus Prayer. I knew there was now no hope except in God, all worldly support had been offered and nothing had been achieved. Prayer was the only way to help.

I wasn't sure of the time when it occurred to me to also ring Father Basil and ask for his prayers. I didn't want to leave James alone but felt a few minutes would be alright. I told the nurse where I was going and asked her to keep an eye on him. I found the monastery number and as I dialled I thought of the other times I had rung him and how different everything had been at those moments: this time it was out of desperation. Father Basil answered and I dropped the coins into the slot and began to blurt out what was happening. His voice was calm but serious, "Trust in God and His Mother," he said, "James will survive."

That last word struck me deeply, at no time had anyone acknowledged the possibility of James dying, but when Father Basil said it I was relieved that my worst fear had been addressed. I kept the conversation short, and thanked him for his prayers. I returned the receiver to its place and leaned against the wall. The worry had drained me and I was exhausted. I shut my eyes tight and begged God to help. I had no one to hope in but Him, every other possible source of strength was now emptied, I knew that our lives were completely dependent on His will.

I headed back to the ward but before I could reach our room the nurse approached me.

"Mr. Lee, you've just missed a visitor, your priest came to visit James." I was surprised to hear this, and asked "Where is he now?"

"He left soon after arriving, he didn't go in to see James, but stood outside the window of the room looking in at him. We allow the clergy to come outside visiting hours, so if you want to have him come back any time, feel free to do so."

I thanked her and wondered why Father Philotheos hadn't stayed to speak to me but was relieved that he had been. I found James in exactly the same position as I had left him, and resumed the bathing of his head. As I touched him I noticed his temperature appeared to have fallen slightly and I took encouragement from it. It wasn't enough to notify the nurse about, but it gave me something to hold on to.

Over the next few hours there was a further drop in James' temperature, and though it was still too high, he no longer felt like he was burning up. I kicked off my shoes and climbed onto the bed beside him taking care not to lie so close as to add any heat to him. I managed to snatch a few hours sleep and each time I woke through the night I emptied the bowl and refreshed it with cold water. At six the next morning I was woken by a different nurse as she entered the room, she gave me a warm smile when she saw me lying with my son. As I sat up James opened his eyes and said "Where are we daddy?"

Fresh tears filled my eyes as I answered him; I placed my hand on his chest and it was a completely normal temperature. The rash had gone and his skin had returned to its normal pink. I swung my legs over the bed and got to my feet as the nurse began removing the needle from his arm.

"We don't need this now, do we James?" To hear her addressing him directly and seeing his curiosity at the tube attached to him felt nothing short of resurrection that he was back amongst us, alive again. I wanted to tell Julie the news but since she would be arriving in an hour or so decided to stay with James. The nurse asked him if he would like some toast and he nodded his head enthusiastically. She brought him a drink and after getting through his first round of toast went on to finish off two more. Every mouthful he took brought me joy; I wanted every ounce of energy and strength to fill his body.

The doctor did a brief examination of him and confirmed that it must have been some other virus and that James was over the worst. When Julie arrived she threw her arms around him in relief, her eyes filling with tears. We chatted a little and I filled her in on the details of the night and the progress of James' recovery. When I told her that Father Philotheos had been she looked confused.

"I rang him again when I got home," she said, "there's no way he could have visited." I couldn't understand what this meant and asked the nurse at the desk about our visitor. I was informed that the nurse who had been on duty at the time wouldn't be back until later that afternoon and I was left having to wait before getting to the bottom of it. We gathered our things and with a little advice from the doctor about how to keep watch over James were told it would be alright to take him home. I drove them back, picked up a change of clothes and managed to make it to work on time. I was tired but satisfied that our world was no longer under immediate threat. After lunch I rang the hospital and was put through to the ward. I recognised the sound of the nurse's voice from the night before and explained that I was trying to work out who our visitor had been.

"Could you describe what he looked like?" I asked.

"He was a tall man, with a long grey beard and a black shawl that came down from his hat."

The whole world seemed to blur around me, as though time had stopped and thrown everything out of focus. The description of Father Basil was unmistakeable, but I knew he had only just spoken to me from the monastery, a journey of over two hours. I thanked her for her help and sat quietly at my desk. Although it was impossible, a part of me knew it was true. It seemed too much to accept, it opened the world up to things I thought I believed but when faced with their reality left me feeling shocked. And yet each time I accepted what was before me a great peace filled my heart. I was struggling with the voices that kept reminding me that this was the twentieth century, the age of computers and rational minds, but the deepest part of me could see reality for what it truly is.

I rang Julie in the afternoon to see how James was doing and she handed the receiver over to him. With great enthusiasm he told me about our neighbour's cat and how it had caught a bird in our garden. His voice sounded strong and I was left in no doubt about his recovery. Julie then informed me that her mother was coming over after she had found out about James. I didn't think it was a good idea to have too many people in the house so soon but it was obvious that the decision had already been made. I wanted to tell her what the nurse had said but couldn't find the words and left it. I decided it would be best to share something like that in person as I wasn't sure how she would react.

That evening I got back to find Julie's mother's car parked outside the house. I wanted to focus entirely on James when I got in and knew things wouldn't be quite that simple, but it was good to be home and I was eager to see my son. Julie kissed me and as she drew her head away her eyes flashed a knowing look that let me know that something was wrong. I sensed I should watch what I said in front of our visitor but I couldn't figure out what the problem was.

I wanted to tell Julie what the nurse had said but felt inhibited by her mother's presence. James ran over to me and I picked him up. He still felt underweight, there was a noticeable difference to him, but his usual character had returned and he was full of energy. I asked him what he had eaten and when he couldn't remember everything Julie's mother filled in the missing details. Julie told me she had kept regular checks on his temperature and that all had been normal. I was confident the virus had left him and the anxiety of the previous day was now completely gone.

Julie prepared dinner while I sat chatting with her mother and James. She asked about my work and various other safe subjects but avoided any talk of church. This was unusual for her as her conversation was normally peppered with details about various events and incidents relating to her Baptist chapel. But the lack of sleep from the previous night had left me exhausted and I didn't pay much attention to much of what she said.

Eventually Julie called us through for our meal and we were faced with a problem. Our usual practice was to sing grace facing our icon corner but we didn't know how our guest might react. In the end it would have left us more uncomfortable not to have sung our prayers and without making a fuss we crossed ourselves and began to pray. Julie's mother fell silent and I avoided looking her way for a while. We passed round the bowls of food and James' observations gave us enough to focus on to not have to mention anything serious. But Julie's mother was preoccupied and wasn't prepared to conceal her concerns.

"Why do you have to pray to those paintings?" Her voice was monotone.

"We don't pray to the icons themselves," said Julie, "but to the ones portrayed in them." She gave her mother a smile in an attempt to lighten the mood but it wasn't returned.

"We don't allow any images of any kind in the chapel, we're very strict about this."

"What about the cross?" Julie said.

"That's not an image, it's a symbol."

"I disagree," Julie continued, "there are plenty of Muslims who accuse Christians of worshipping the cross like a pagan idol."

"That's deeply offensive Julie, how can you even say that?"

"Obviously I'm not saying I think that, but I'm just saying the cross is an image. it's not like the Baptists don't allow any image."

"The Baptists!" Julie's mother repeated the words with simmering anger. "I remember when you considered yourself one of those Baptists. Now you're praying in front of pictures. I'm sorry Julie, but you know how we feel about this."

"When do you think the Baptists appeared in the world mother?"

"What do you mean?" Her mother said.

"Think about it, you're always talking about the original Church, assuming that your house groups represent what the first Christians were like. But it's not true mom, the early Church was liturgical, they had bishops and priests."

"That's nonsense Julie, I do not believe that."

"Of course it's true," Julie was managing to remain calm as she spoke, "the Apostles all became bishops. Who do you think it was who decided on the canon of the New Testament? It was the bishops of the Church. The Orthodox Church is the continuation of that same Church from the first century. That's why I ask when the Baptists came into existence. How can you claim to be the original Church if you've only existed for four hundred years? It doesn't make any sense."

"The Church was led astray by the popes, but the true Christian faith was kept alive by real Christians who have always existed."

"First of all the popes belong to Rome, they separated themselves off from the Church, just like the Protestants. We don't feel any need to explain or excuse the behaviour of Rome. It has nothing to do with us."

I had remained silent, I wasn't confident enough in our relationship to start arguing with her. But I couldn't hold my tongue any more. "The fruits of the Church are the saints," I said. "If you want to know where God's Spirit is at work you only need look for signs of holiness. The Church's history is full of the most incredible saints."

Julie's mother turned to me for the first time and as she began to speak I realised how much she blamed me for leading her daughter astray.

"We have many manifestations of the Holy Spirit Stewart. I'm sure you've read the Book of Acts, well, speaking in tongues continues today. Julie knows I speak in tongues, it is a great blessing for me."

"What does it do for you?" I asked.

"It is God's way of allowing my spirit to worship Him in a higher way, a more spiritual way."

"In the Book of Acts the Apostles spoke in the languages of the various visitors to Jerusalem, it was a sign that the gospel was to be preached to all nations. Which language do you speak in?" I knew my question was confrontational, but I was tired and irritated.

"I have been blessed to speak in the tongue of angels." With this pronouncement Julie's mother darted a look of victory at her daughter. The arrogance of this statement left me wanting nothing more of the conversation. Julie tried to remain patient, "How do you know what it means? Who interprets what you're saying?"

"I don't have messages for the congregation; I speak in tongues in worship. This doesn't need translating because it is between me and God."

I didn't want to be rude, but I wanted to tell her that I believed it was a false religion she belonged to, that the signs she clung to had no similarity with the manifestations of God's power in the Church: that ultimately I believed she was being misled by her own ego and possibly worse. Julie had described to me the way the Baptist congregations had worked themselves into an emotional ecstasy and I knew it was no more than spiritual sensuality, a desire for experiences and signs.

"Are you saying God no longer works miracles in our age Stewart?"

"No, I'm not saying that," I fought the urge to describe what had happened at the hospital, "we believe the power of God is very much at work in our world. How else could there be any goodness in any of us?"

The conversation came to an abrupt end and we finished our food. James was aware of the atmosphere and fell silent too. It was a relief to finally leave the table and occupy myself with the day's post. I could hear Julie and her mother chatting in the other room and though there was still an edge to their voices they had moved on to more mundane matters. After a coffee we walked Julie's mother to her car and she mechanically gave each of us a kiss on the cheek. It felt forced and I was glad to see her driving away.

Inside the house I said "Are you alright?"

"Yea, don't worry, I know how she feels. It's not a problem for me."

I could see she meant it. "I spoke to the nurse from last night."

"What did she say?"

"I know this is going to sound crazy, but she described Father Basil. But I had only just spoken to him on the 'phone."

"Why don't you ask him? Be straight with him, what have you got to lose?"

I thought about her suggestion for a moment, it was the obvious, logical thing to do. But I was nervous about it; I didn't know how I might react or what it would mean if he confirmed our suspicion. It was one thing to think such a thing might be possible, but I wasn't sure I was ready to have him confirm it.

Julie could see my uncertainty and said "What are you afraid of?"

1989

As the next few months passed after James' illness I began to forget about the mysterious incident with Father Basil. Forget is not really the right word, it didn't completely slip from my mind, but I began to be less affected by its memory. As time went by I even began to doubt the order of events and wondered if my memory could be trusted. I remembered how tired I had been, how stressful the whole situation had felt, and slowly my rational mind began to erase any possibility of anything miraculous having taken place. It wasn't that I didn't want to believe in such things, I was firmly convinced in the truth of miracles, but this was all a little too close to home. So I managed to push the thought from my mind. Anyone who argues that they would believe in God if only they could see some sign or wondrous event is wrong. Faith doesn't grow from such spectacles, even Jesus refused to perform signs to satisfy men's need of "proof". And so I gently moved on and allowed the event to fade in importance.

Even as I drove to the monastery I had no pressing questions to raise, no explanation I had urgent need of, I felt only the usual excitement at the prospect of seeing the monks. Father Seraphim greeted me at the door, and I received the typical monastic welcome. He brought refreshments and sat to talk while Father Basil attended to something in the chapel.

"How are you all?" I asked.

"We continue to be blessed; we have a new Father from Greece, Father Isaac." It was good to hear that the monastery was growing; it gave me a sense of reassurance. Without any thought I said "I sometimes envy your life here."

Father Seraphim looked at me quite sternly and said "This is a trick the devil plays on us. Be careful not to envy our life here too much."

I was surprised by the comment, and felt a need to explain myself. "I didn't mean anything by it Father."

"The devil attacks us all," he continued. "Into the minds of men who are married he suggests thoughts of heroic struggles in a monastery. He suggests to married men that they would be better off without the distractions of a wife and family, without all the practical problems of life which get in the way of prayer. But then into the ears of young men who enter the monastic life he whispers complaints about the loneliness of being a monk, he suggests they would be better off with a loving wife. You see how the devil breeds dissatisfaction in anyone who will listen? We must pay him no attention and accept the place in life that God gives us. Heaven is filled with saints from monastic and married lives; no one should think their place in the world can exclude them from God's grace. The task set before all of us is to take the struggles and temptations God permits us and use them as opportunities to draw closer to Him."

The regret at having said the wrong thing left me and I was thankful for his guidance. "Should we see all our struggles in this way Father?"

"Of course. Only when we suffer, when we feel we are lost do we truly know our need of God. The rich man who has everything the world can give feels no need of God. But this is an illusion; his riches have blinded him from the truth of his situation. This is why Christ warned us about the camel passing through the eye of a needle, because the rich man has no desire to enter Heaven, he thinks he has found it on earth. The riches and pleasures of this world are snares, we must be careful not to allow them to catch us."

"I am often caught by these snares, Father; I find my work encourages me to think in a very worldly way."

"We cannot blame our work, but if it really is something that prevents you from being perfected you must find something else to do. It is only for a short while; this life is a brief moment in time. As long as you can support your family do not imagine it as of any great importance. Some work can be very beneficial to others, and some men are called to great tasks, but most of us are far more mundane than this."

I remembered the words Father Basil had spoken to me years before and wasn't sure if Father Seraphim was contradicting him. "What about men's calling by God?" I said.

"We should not confuse our own desire for things with God's calling, but neither should we dismiss our feelings when God gives us a genuine desire for something good. God calls us in many ways, sometimes just by presenting a need before us. We shouldn't look for special signals, but see God's hand in all things, even in the little things of life. When we recognise that God is intimately involved in our lives we have a better sense of how He is helping us and how He is challenging us. When we live in this awareness we are living the true life we were created for. The danger is that we look for big signs, clear signals from God, because we have lost sight of His intimate involvement in all things. It is really one more consequence of our unrestrained ego – we imagine we are worthy of special signs because we feel we are so important. Of course, the truth is we are not. "

The door opened and Father Basil came in. I was startled to see his beard had turned completely white and his youthful face looked tired and strained. But his smile was a constant and it was a joy to be greeting him.

"Welcome to the monastery Stewart, how are things?" I briefly mentioned a few details and he said "How's James?"

The question reminded me of his illness the previous year and as I assured him that James was in good health I remembered the night at the hospital. I hesitated to ask him about it, and before I could speak Father Basil said "God's love for our children is very great. We must let the name of our children be on our lips when we speak to God even more often than God's name should be on our lips when we speak to our children. As they grow up parents should never harangue them or create conflict. I am not saying they should not discipline then when necessary, but when it comes to teaching the faith we must teach by example rather than by words. We cannot morally bully our children into being good Christians. Again and again bring them to God and His mother in your prayers and put your trust in their care. Too many parents feel they can force their children into a knowledge of God but the truth is such a relationship only grows when they meet God and learn to love Him. Parents must pray for their children, day after day, God will hear these prayers and answer them."

Father Seraphim excused himself and left and I felt the time was right to ask my questions. "Father, when James was ill last year something happened that I'm not sure about, I.."

I felt awkward asking him about it. But he didn't allow me to continue, he said "Often we place great significance in the wrong things and through them miss what is really important. You must thank God for healing James; this is the truth of what happened. He was very ill but God restored him to health. God heard our prayers, all of our prayers; this is the only important fact in what happened."

I could see he wouldn't be drawn on anything further and that I had to drop the subject. He asked

"How is your prayer? Are you managing to find time to pray each day?"

"We pray every evening Father, but there are other things on my mind. I have people at work I find it difficult to get along with, and even when I'm praying I find them popping into my head. How do I find peace about this?"

"Often the problem can be that we know we have offended somebody or they have offended us. In either case forgiveness is necessary. If they have offended you then you must pray for them and genuinely forgive them. If you know you have wronged them then you must take it to God in your confession."

"But how do I change my feelings towards them?"

"You must perform small acts of mercy, small acts of compassion towards them. Always be watching for ways that you can help or serve them. Do not be too obvious, but discreetly do what you can to help them in every way possible. Even if you do not feel like doing this it will have a great effect on you. It is one of the ways we change our hearts when they are dead. Through our actions we are able to transform our inner self; such acts of kindness bring great healing to our hearts. But do not do anything with resentment, this is of benefit to no one."

His face was full of concern and care and I knew that nothing he said was out of judgement, but came from the wisdom of his experience in his own spiritual struggles. He looked at me not as a judge, but as a co-defendant who had once stood facing the same assaults of an accuser and had learned how to defeat every charge.

"All that we do helps to bring life to our soul," he said. "Eternal life is not ours by right; we do not have it by nature. Eternal life comes to the soul as it is illuminated with the light of Christ. Through the process of theosis we are given eternal life. Each little act of kindness that we perform, especially to those who have offended us, is a step towards perfection. Forget the great acts of mystics and those who claim to work miracles, this is not our concern. We work at our perfection in the relationships God gives us. By forgiving and trying to love one another we achieve everything. And this can only be done if we unite ourselves to Christ in prayer. It is all very uncomplicated, so simple even a child can understand it. Seek to serve God by serving your neighbour, see the image of God in every man and know that when you serve a friend or stranger you serve God."

The questions I had felt needed answering now seemed silly and unnecessary. My desire for answers had been motivated by the same kind of feelings that prompt people to want to hear prophecies and speak in tongues; it was nothing truly spiritual, only one more craving, a kind of spiritual gluttony. As I listened to him speak it was like clear running water that refreshed and cleansed me and satisfied every appetite.

"Western man has lost sense of himself in all his fullness," he continued. "You will often hear people speak about false ideas or confused thinking. But the heart is subject to its own forms of delusions. Western man has lost sight of this reality and so does nothing to correct or protect himself in these matters. We must light a fire in the heart and burn out the false and evil occupants. The passions are a destructive army that offer us no pleasure when we unite ourselves to Christ. Compassion and forgiveness are the sweetest joys to a heart given to God, but sadly too many hearts in this part of the world are filled with the dark pleasures that Satan convinces them will bring satisfaction."

"But how do we learn to distinguish between the two?" I asked.

"We must train the heart to taste and love what is true. We can only do this by participating fully in the life of the Church. The cycles and seasons are very important, but what is absolutely essential is that we receive Holy Communion and confess our sins. These are the heavenly tools with which the Church brings us God's healing. It is healing from the wounds of darkness, from the passions, from all that Satan throws at us. When healing comes to us through the sacraments we are bathed in God's light, we are surrounded by angels, the inner chambers of our being become illuminated until eventually there are no dark corners in which Satan can hide. It is a fire which burns all impurity, and as we know it can be painful. But like the fire that burned the bush before Moses, it does not destroy us. God is in the fire, we must allow Him to ignite our hearts. It brings a warmth that we can feel, a real warmth in the heart, that radiates love and peace so that we become free to love even as God loves. Once the fire burns pure within us we become this fire, it transforms us into flame so that not just our hearts but our minds, our words, everything becomes light. This is theosis; it is the perfection every man was born to know."

Realising he was saying more than he intended he looked at me to gauge my reaction. He added "And we strike the sparks through kindness and love. All of us, however long we have been stoking this fire, must never ignore the need for little sparks. We must approach it as if it is new every day, so that it feels like we are lighting the fire from scratch. We must never imagine that the fire is raging sufficiently within us that we can walk away and allow it to burn of its own accord, or sit back and enjoy its comforts. We must work hard all our lives to keep striking the little sparks and leave the great fire of illumination to the Holy Spirit. This way we avoid falling into pride which is the worst delusion the heart can fall into and which pulls us into a darkness deeper than any other. An angel of light fell from heaven because of pride, who are we to imagine our selves immune?"

"I find that when my work or other people affect me I have little enthusiasm for what I know is really important. I become focussed on all the wrong things and give in to my weaknesses." As I spoke I was expressing my feelings as much to myself as to him.

"Our attraction to the things of this life inhibits our spiritual growth. When we become downcast we begin to seek comfort in material things and this can lead to destruction. Once the physical man becomes more important than the needs of the soul we find ourselves living with a tyrant. The simple needs of the body are multiplied by bad habits so that even basic things like food, shelter and clothing become obsessions for people. I see people in the West who franticly run to satisfy these natural needs to the point where their whole being is preoccupied with what should be no more than a basic requirement. As they pursue these material pleasures they sink deeper into a state of sensuality until they completely neglect everything spiritual, leaving them with a hunger that is never satisfied. The body is pampered but the soul goes hungry. They are victims of their own weakness but also of the manipulation by companies wanting to sell them things. Advertising stimulates everything that is base and dark in people, it encourages craving and desire. Modern man is bound by the dark chains of consumerism, he is attacked by the television, newspapers, even when he travels images and slogans surround him. The mind is bombarded by a satanic world-view that ceaselessly works to plant seeds of materialism into him. As soon as a person is tired or neglectful these seeds grow until the victim is powerless to cut them down. I frequently meet people who are confused and lost in life because they live in the spiritual turmoil of western atheism."

"But isn't this a problem all over the world?" I asked.

"It is becoming more widespread as globalisation increases. The corporations are spreading their influence into every corner of the globe, backed by banking and military power. The politicians are no more than puppets; it is power and money which pulls the strings. But mankind is only vulnerable to these powers so long as it participates in the programmes set before it, the materialistic philosophies. While there are people alive who hold on to the truth then Satan can never have complete control. Christ promised that the Church would hold out even to the very end of time, it will be attacked, it will shrink to a small number, but there will always be a grain of faith – sufficient for hope to remain alive."

"People have always thought they are living at the end of time Father, the facts of history have always made people think the end is near. What are we to think today?"

His face grew very serious, "Christ told us to watch and understand. No one knows the hour or the day, not even the angels, and when you hear any group proclaiming a date or that they have some special revelation before the event, shun them. Have nothing to do with such people for they are deluded and dangerous. But at the same time we must follow our Lord's command to be watchful, to read the times around us. I do not say that we are about to see the end of the world, but the world is changing, the time is nearly right for Anti-Christ."

A shiver ran through me as he said this, I had never heard him speak of these issues before and it wasn't something I associated with his teaching.

"There is a push for a one world government; it has never been possible for man to arrange his affairs this way before." He continued to speak slowly, carefully choosing his words to express his points without ambiguity. "Only when men have set the scene will Anti-Christ appear, but we see the foundations being laid already. It may be in our lifetime, or in your children's, it may be another hundred years, but there is an acceleration in the world's slide to darkness. Men are losing love for God and one another. We see society glorifying evil, applauding selfishness and greed. There is an abandonment of God's law so that men do as they will in the name of freedom and equality. Man is becoming ruthless and turning away from the image of God within him. Humanity will soon be unrecognisable, and all the time man tells himself he is evolving, becoming more sophisticated and superior to the men of the past. It is a demonic lie, and those who stand against it are persecuted. Yes, the signs are all around us, but we must remain sober in our thinking. We must not panic or work ourselves into a frenzy. Stay focussed on the simple demands of life; as long as we persist in our simple pursuit of God we will remain safe. Even if they break and burn our bodies, God will not forsake us. But always remember that peace and true satisfaction cannot be found through the things of this world. The moment we trust in earthly comforts or securities we are heading in the wrong direction. If we imagine that wealth and power are the answer to anything, then we are blind. We are living in a world run by the blind and anyone who claims to be able to see is a threat to their deception. Do not put your trust in their promises, or on their prizes, or in yourself. If you trust in anything it becomes an idol and separates you from God. We must give our hearts completely to Him, holding nothing back, without lifeboat or safety net, we must trust in Him and set out without anything to fall back on. When we do this He meets us, protects us, He guides us by walking with us and we discover that there was never anything to fear all along."

I could sense my heart warming to his words but somewhere within me I felt it was different for monks than it was for the rest of us. He smiled and said "Do you think your house or your work is anything to keep you from complete union with God? On the contrary, all things can be used to lead us closer to Him. It is not only the time we monks spend in prayer that God rewards. Every time you choose patience, every fair dealing you have in your business, everything you do in life that is performed in service of God is redeemed by Christ and becomes a means of your own redemption. Relatively few men are called to live on mountains, but all men are called to live in Paradise. God sends us every opportunity we need to be perfected; every day for every one of us is filled with chances to respond to God's calling. We simply need to raise our eyes from the materialism that pulls us down and recognise the truth of our lives. Every person we meet is brought to us by God. Every encounter we have, even the brief interaction at the supermarket till, provides us with the opportunity to treat another human being with respect, a chance to see the divine dignity placed there by God. When we truly believe that all men are created in God's image the whole world is transformed for us. The crowds that pass us in the street become a wonder, a glorious glimpse into Heaven. We must look beyond the frailty and failings of men, just as we ask God to see beyond our own sinfulness, we must look to the perfect image of Christ in every man and woman that we are blessed to see."

I was beginning to see the world through his eyes, beginning to sense how he felt about me and every other pilgrim that interrupted his silence here in the monastery. But above all I was acutely aware of God's presence with us. The undeniable, tangible presence of the One Who made and loved us. Father Basil had led my consciousness, my mind and heart to a place where I could begin to perceive reality without the shackles with which I had willingly bound myself. A deep peace filled me as it filled the room and the whole world around us. The very stone of the walls, the wood of the furniture and our physical being was lifted out of a dull materialism into a reality that was both familiar and new. As I looked into his face I felt my heart surrounded in his prayers and knew that God's love flowed out to me through him. The whole room began to brighten with a light that had no specific visible source and from within Father Basil there emanated a golden light that was unlike any earthly light I had ever seen.

He smiled, as though he knew exactly what I was seeing, and as I watched his lips mouthing the words of the Jesus Prayer I felt it being spoken within me. There was no sound coming from him but my heart seemed to be in time with the rhythm of his prayer, as though his heart was marking the pattern of prayer for my own.

"You must know that the whole creation is connected to your heart. When the Holy Trinity dwells within us we find the unity of the whole universe." His face began to resume its normal appearance and I felt my thoughts and perceptions returning to their normal, inhibited manner. I was already beginning to inwardly question what had happened when he broke my line of thought.

"You must make sure Julie eats plenty of broccolis."

I had no idea what he meant by this, it caught me off guard and left me a little confused. Without explaining any further he stood up and gathered the tea cups together. He carried them through to the kitchen and I could hear the sound of him washing up. I glanced at my watch and was surprised at how much time had passed. As he returned he said "You must think about heading back before it starts getting dark." I agreed and found my coat. He saw me to the door and I thanked him for his words.

"You must pray for me," he said, "always know that God hears your prayers. Pray for the world Stewart, people everywhere need our prayers now more than ever before."

Over dinner that night Julie was keen to hear about everything that had happened at the monastery. I downplayed my impression of what I had seen, but went into as much detail as I could remember about what Father Basil had said. She kept prompting me to recall details I might have overlooked and listened very seriously throughout. When I finally came to his remark about the broccoli she gave me a broad smile, "I'm going to have another baby," she said. "He knew."

2014

From 1990 onwards Father Basil's involvement with the Church in Romania extended to his help with the establishment of two new monasteries and also an orphanage which he visited each year. The fall of Communism enabled fresh links to be developed between the traditional Orthodox peoples of the former Eastern Block and the growing Orthodox presence in the West. English speaking Orthodox parishes began to appear up and down the country, comprising congregations of immigrants and English converts such as our selves. There was an increasing sense of momentum as the Church grew, as new clergy were ordained and as more people discovered the true nature of what so many in Britain had previously called the "Celtic tradition". It came as a surprise to many people to discover that Britain had long been an Orthodox nation before the Normans brought Roman Catholicism to these lands.

As our annual visits to the monastery continued we noticed greater numbers of pilgrims finding their way to Father Basil's door. The monastery guest house was enlarged and Father Basil made himself available to all who asked for his time. Sometimes fifty or sixty people would arrive at his door in a single day and for all he had time and concern. After the Church of England voted to ordain women ministers in 1992 a steady stream of Anglican clergy began to enquire about conversion:

but most continued to look elsewhere once they discovered they would be accepted only as laymen and that any hope of ordination was to a priesthood that brought no financial reward.

Father Basil gave of himself beyond his physical endurance and inevitably his health began to suffer. The long hours in church combined with his care of pilgrims began to take their toll and it was noticeable how much he was physically changing from visit to visit. His beard had become white as snow, and his once tall, youthful frame became bent as his back developed problems. But he never complained and was always focussed on the needs and complaints of his visitors.

We now had three children and were already thinking about retirement from work. The possibility of having more time on our hands meant we would be able to visit the monastery more frequently and perhaps become more involved with our local parish. We often talked in this way about the future, the children had left home and it seemed we were at last going to be doing more of what we wanted rather than what life demanded that we do.

It was a Sunday night in June when I answered the telephone. Hearing Father Seraphim's voice I was immediately concerned, no one from the monastery had ever called us before. His voice was sombre and before he could speak I guessed what was coming.

"Father Basil has died; I am letting people know so that you can pray for him."

"When did he die Father?"

"Last night, he had taken to his bed a few days before, but he grew very weak and there was noting the doctors could do for him."

"When is the funeral Father?"

"It will be on Tuesday morning, you are most welcome to come."

"I'll be there, thank you for letting me know Father."

He gave me details of the service but said the guest house was already booked. The call was brief; he had a number of other people to contact, and so brought the conversation to a quick end.

I wandered through to Julie who was sitting in her armchair reading.

"What's wrong?" She asked.

"Father Basil has died!"

Her eyes filled with tears and she stood to embrace me. We held each other for a moment; there was nothing we could say to express our loss.

"The funeral's the day after tomorrow, I'll drive up early in the morning. Will you be able to get off work?"

"I'll ask," she said, "will you be able to sort the time off?"

"I don't care what they might say. I'm going to call in sick; I'm not going to risk them saying no."

We sat facing each other, aware that our world suddenly felt very different. "That was Father Seraphim; he didn't give many details about how he died."

"He hasn't looked well for some time, we've both noticed it," said Julie.

"I know, but I thought he'd go on for ever, I never imagined he'd be gone."

We began to recall our visits and it was a comfort to sit sharing memories of him. It took us back to our days at university and we recounted our first impressions that day of the lecture. It also brought back to me the image of Julie in her early twenties; it didn't seem possible that we could be sitting here so close to old age. The brevity of our lives is a cliché all young people hear about but only when the decades have stacked up does its reality come into focus. It had been nearly forty years since we first met him, his influence on us had been beyond measure, and now he was dead.

Despite Father Seraphm's request, we didn't pray for Father Basil that night. We allowed too much sentimentality to cloud our thinking and failed to do the one thing necessary. The next day at work I hinted at feeling unwell and by the end of the day had created enough of an impression to support the lie I would be delivering the following day. Julie however, was more honest and was rewarded with a refusal to go. They were short-handed where she worked and she was needed for her shift. She came home very angry and I tried to comfort her.

The alarm clock rang at five on Tuesday morning but I was already awake. I had had a restless night, troubled by the thought of his death. In truth it was more a realisation that our own end was closer than we dared to think and I knew I wasn't ready to face it. Even in my sixties I felt that life had barely begun properly, that the brief flash of time had passed before I had done everything that needed to be achieved. It wasn't a list of unfulfilled worldly ambitions that played on my mind, but a realisation that I had been lazy in my prayers, that I hadn't loved or forgiven as I should, that my heart was too often a dead stone that rarely radiated the presence of Christ. The thought of death didn't bring fear, only shame and regret. When I looked back at my life I knew I would have very little to show for myself when it was time to stand before God. The holy death of someone like Father Basil was very different to how my conclusion would be.

The roads were quiet and I made good time. I had brought a camera at Julie's request and was wondering how appropriate it would really be to start taking photographs on a day like this. With such nonsense filling my head I turned into the final stretch of lane. There were cars already parked along the side of the hedge leaving just enough room for a single vehicle to pass. I found a gap and manoeuvred my way into the line. It was a cool morning but the sun was bright making everything around me look beautiful. As I walked I noticed the birdsong, the blossom on the trees, the squirrels darting from branch to branch. All around me the world was alive, it continued to live as it always had, and yet up ahead of me lay the body of our friend. The impact of his death was not in the orbits of planets or the moving of clouds, it was far more pronounced: the importance of his death was in our hearts. His meaning was in people and before God. There were no visible signs to mark his passing, but none were necessary: nothing superficial was needed to validate the event. The world could continue on as it always had but for those who loved him everything was different.

As I approached the monastery gate I could see groups of people standing around in conversation. There were many priests and monks amongst them, and as I drew closer to the monastery building I realised there were further groups behind the house. With the exception of about half a dozen of them all were men. I made my way to the church where a marquee extension had been added to the building to provide shelter for the many that wouldn't be able to fit inside for the service. The church was busy and at the centre of the crowd was Father Basil's open coffin. A choir of monks was chanting psalms and despite everyone milling around there was already a prayerful atmosphere. I pressed forwards and found myself looking down into Father Basil's face. The creases of pain had left him and his face looked serene. It hardly seemed possible but he looked to be smiling. On his chest was laid an icon of the Theotokos and besides this there was a large wooden cross. For the first time since I had heard news of his death I felt able to pray for him. I thanked God for everything that Father Basil meant to us and with great confidence prayed that he find a place with God. Though dead, his physical remains were a clear link to him; this was not some shell to be cast off like an unwanted garment. Father Basil's soul was mysteriously connected with his body and to be close to it brought us closer to him in Heaven. I had no doubts of any kind about this; here was a tangible link to the unseen world that had been sanctified through the years of spiritual labours. It was not only Father Basil's soul that God's grace had made holy, but his physical remains too. As we gathered to honour him, we would do so here in this world, treating his body with great dignity as a means of honouring the soul that lived in the next. Like the veneration performed before an icon, his body was now our means of contact to his eternal condition.

I moved to the back of the crowd and out into the fresh air. A man in his early thirties smiled and asked if I had come far. We began to exchange stories about our encounters with Father Basil and I realised that most of the people around us were doing the same thing.

"I was addicted to drugs when I first met Father Basil," he said. "My life was in a terrible mess but he gave me the strength to trust in God. I am sure I would be dead now if I hadn't met him."

I understood the emotion behind his words, just as many people there could have recounted the great debt they owed to this man of God.

"I have seen people arrive for the first time and Father Basil not only knew their names but also what their problems were. People would just give him lists of names and he would be able to pray for each as though they had been personally to visit him. Such men are rare," he continued. "We are blessed to have known him. God has brought each of us into contact with him for our benefit; God has made His grace known to us through Father Basil."

I told him I agreed. It was a comfort to be around people who shared my loss; it helped me to see beyond my own personal concerns to what was really happening. We had been there for about twenty minutes when a number of vested priests processed into church. A deep baritone voice began to sing to which the large choir responded. The service had begun and from outside we could hear the bells of the censors as clouds of sweet smoke began to drift out to us. The Church's voice began to lament a soul's passing and then called out to God for mercy.

There was movement in church as people began to move to the coffin. Each person in turn bent and kissed the head of Father Basil. The queue was loose and disorganised but eventually I was moving in through the door of the church. After another ten minutes I stepped to the head of the coffin and once more gazed in at his peaceful expression. A veil had been placed over his forehead and slowly I bent and pressed my lips against it. It was an act of great intimacy and for the first time I began to weep. But the tears were sweet, an unexpected joy mixed in with the grief.

I stepped to one side and managed to occupy a space in the corner of the church. From here I watched as the priests prayed the ancient words that have marked the end of countless lives. Through the centuries of humanity these same prayers have been offered for frail men and women who have struggled against temptation. For both holy saints and unrepentant sinners, the Church has called on God for forgiveness. And the whole congregation knew only too well that the moment lay ahead when a choir would gather to sing over their death. Each of us found our mortality brought into clear focus and understood, at least for a while, that the value of life is only discovered by those who live with an awareness of death. At that moment there was nothing more important anywhere on earth than the singing of those hymns, words that called on God to fulfil Hs promises.

The lid was eventually placed on the coffin and a group of monks including Father Seraphim and Father John lifted it and carried it out to an area of land that had been newly fenced off. The priests slowly led the way and we followed, standing quietly as the coffin was lowered into the grave. The hole of black soil was uneven and fresh; there was nothing reassuring about it. The priests and choir continued to sing and with his body now hidden from sight there was a sense that his journey had truly come to an end. Without any fuss the monks and clergy began to walk away from the grave and the congregation was left wondering what to do next. We began to wander back towards the house and there we found the monks had laid out three long tables from which they were serving coffee. A number of short queues formed and the monks served everyone with great efficiency.

I took my cup and sat on one of the benches that had been provided. Father Seraphim noticed me and came over to join me.

"It's good to see so many people," I observed.

"Yes, Father Basil touched many lives. He suffered terribly before he died."

"What was he suffering from Father?"

"He was haemorrhaging at the end and despite his great pain he refused any medication to ease his suffering. We didn't know how much pain he was in until after he died when the doctor told us. He had insisted that the doctor keep quiet about it because he knew we would plead with him to accept the pain killers. Of course, he was protecting us too; he did not want us to see him in such pain. There was not a single word of complaint that passed his lips. He suffered with great patience and humility, just as he had lived."

"He was a holy man," I commented rather pointlessly.

"He was a saint, he is a saint!" Father Seraphim's declaration was delivered with absolute certainty. "The night he died we were praying over him, some of the fathers began to notice a sweet smell.

One or two began to mention it and all agreed that they had smelt it. Father Basil gave us a sign that he has been accepted by God as a saint, he gave us that scent to relieve our sorrows and strengthen our faith. Even in death he comforted us"

I was unsure how to react, and said "Do you think he will be recognised as a saint by the wider Church?"

"It is not necessary for the whole world to recognise the truth, it changes nothing. God's saints are in Paradise whether bishops acknowledge it or not. I intend to paint an icon of Father Basil this year. Though I will not publicise the fact, we will perhaps add him to the wall of saints in our church." The thought of Father Basil standing beside the saints he had so often prayed with from this world made sense and I trusted the monks in their judgement.

"Death is not as it should be," said Father Seraphim. "The death of one of God's children is not His will. He created us for life, and has done everything to bring life back to us. But Father Basil and all of us will rise on the final day; death no longer has us in its power. This is our faith Stewart; this is the only truth that makes sense of our life when we look into the graves of our loved ones. We will see Father Basil again, but for now he prays for us before the throne of God. He carries his love for us into Paradise, and the prayers of God's saints are powerful. Grace gives power to the holy, and none are so holy as those who stand before God in Heaven."

As the afternoon moved on people began drifting back to their cars and I decided to head back my self. The monastery buildings looked just as they always did, but now Father Basil's body was a permanent reminder of the purity that could be achieved in this crucible of souls. He was proof of what every man could find, but something few of us want enough to actually achieve. His achievement resulted from faith and a pure desire for God. He had defended his soul from the snares of the world and spent his life protecting his fellow pilgrims. I carried these thoughts away from the monastery, and despite Father Seraphim's confidence, I was burdened with one other thought: "Now he is gone."

2015

For almost a year after his death we tried to adjust to the idea that there would be no more visits to receive his counsel. The annual trips had punctuated our married life and now the anticipation and preparation was gone. At a time in our lives when we hoped things would become more settled we faced one problem after another and Julie in particular was beginning to fall into periods of anxiety. The pension we had assumed was coming our way had collapsed due to mismanagement and we were facing years of work long after we had hoped to be retired. There was a general air of uncertainty about our situation that had caught us unprepared.

After another night discussing what we were going to do I drank a couple of beers and sat alone in the kitchen leaning slumped over the dinner table. Seeing the empty bottles before me Julie barked "You'll snore now, I'm sleeping in the spare room." I offered no resistance, it was her usual response if I drank alcohol and I didn't read any significance into it. I glanced at the clock and realised I had let myself stay up too late; the early morning would take its revenge if I didn't get to bed. I pulled myself to my feet and headed up the stairs.

I had been sleeping for a few hours when suddenly I found myself wide awake. In my dream I had seen Father Basil; he had looked at me and raised his hand to point. I couldn't see where he was pointing but somehow I knew he was indicating the direction of the monastery. It had been intensely vivid but even as it happened I was aware that I was still asleep. He had a look of utter peace, and when I woke I wanted nothing more than to be back in the dream. I lay awake in the dark thinking about the times we had spent with him and in this condition I drifted happily back to sleep.

In the morning I was sitting back at the table nursing my tea. Julie appeared in her dressing gown and sat opposite me. She leaned over the table and placed her hands over mine.

"You okay?" I asked. "Can't you sleep?"

"I had a dream about Father Basil last night," she said.

I froze at her words and my own dream came back to me. "I dreamt about him too."

She didn't react in any way to my statement; I waited for her to say something.

"Father Basil told me .."

"He spoke to you?" I said cutting her off.

She nodded, "Yes. He told me we should visit him, he meant go to the monastery. What happened in your dream?"

"He pointed to the monastery, but didn't say anything."

"That's not all he said to me," she took my cup and drank a sip of my tea. "He said we must pray to the Theotokos."

"We do," I insisted.

"Yes, but he was insistent, I knew he was urging us to pray to her more."

"What do you think this means?" I said.

"Obviously we have to visit his grave at the monastery," she was a little curt in her tone.

"No, I don't mean that. What does it mean that we both had dreams about him on the same night? It's more than a coincidence."

"Of course it's not a coincidence; I can't believe you're even saying that. He visited us Stewart, he was here."

I knew she was right and I didn't understand why a part of me was resistant to it.

"Ring the monastery when you get home from work Stewart, we need to go soon."

It was two weeks later when we made the trip. We hadn't spoken again about our dreams but it was something never far from my thoughts. It was a relief to finally be doing what we both believed he had told us to do. The monastery had returned to its atmosphere of stillness and all traces of that busy day the previous year had vanished. As we approached the front door we could see the new graveyard and Julie insisted that we go over before alerting the monks to our presence.

A low gate had been installed but visitors could just as easily have stepped over the fence which existed to mark the area rather than keep anyone out. The single wooden cross stood in the corner at the head of a raised mound of earth. Father Basil's name was written in Romanian and I was struck by how far he had come from his nation of birth. It hardly seemed possible that the face, the hands, the very physical being he had occupied now lay beneath that soil. I had seen the coffin lowered but now it all looked so different.

We stood quietly at the head of the grave, wanting to pray but not sure of what to say. In the end Julie said aloud "Thank you Lord for Father Basil, grant him peace."

Behind us and unseen Father Seraphim had walked over and he only caught my eye as he began to cross himself.

"Hello Father, how are you?" I asked.

"All is well, thank you. The monastery is growing and God is watching over us."

He paused for a moment and added "It is good that you have come to visit Father Basil, it has been a long time."

"We weren't sure how things would be, it's good to be here Father," I assured him.

"And may I ask, what prompted you to come now rather than at another time?" His question seemed to invite us to share something, and I wondered if he was prompting us to tell him about our dreams. I would have once discarded such thoughts as fanciful, but now I was learning to accept a different view of the world.

It was Julie who answered, "Father Basil told us to come."

"I see," said Father Seraphim, "then it is good that you have been obedient."

"He visited us in dreams just a few weeks ago," Julie continued to explain, "we aren't completely sure why."

Father Seraphim thought for a moment, "You must venerate him."

Julie and I looked at each other, we were used to venerating saints of course, but to pray to someone we had known, a person time has not removed from the flesh and blood and all too human reality was new to us.

"There is no doubt in our minds that Father Basil could be anywhere but with God. Both before and since his death God has worked many miracles through his intercessions. He is a saint and we were touched by his holiness, it is unthinkable that he would be anywhere but in Paradise. Do you think his love for you has come to an end? Of course not, he loves you now more than ever before. And one way he expressed his love was through prayer. Do you think he has stopped praying for you? Of course not, and just as you sought his help in this world, you must do so now that he lives in the next. Christ has destroyed the power of death; it no longer clings to us. Death has not ended your friendship with Father Basil; turn to him as you did so many times before. Come with me, I want to show you something."

He turned and began to walk away. We followed him in to the church and he handed us a candle each.

"There, look!" Father Seraphim pointed to our right and before us stood a life-size icon of Father Basil. It was framed but stood beside the frescoes of the saints he had spent so many hours praying with in the past, but had now joined in a more profound way. I lit my candle and placed it in the sand before his icon; the flame's reflection shimmered in the gold behind him. As I looked I knew I was seeing into the reality he now enjoyed, the icon spoke directly to my heart and told me he was in Heaven. The iconographer had captured his slight smile and the physical image immediately brought me into the spiritual reality of his presence. I crossed myself and bowed low, and then drawing close kissed the image of his hand.

"Holy Saint Basil," I whispered, "pray for us."

I stepped back and Julie venerated him. The face in the icon was exactly as it had appeared to us in our dreams, and as I stood before him I felt his prayers lifting my worldly worries from my shoulders. Nothing could affect us, we were drawn into the deeper space that exists within us, the Kingdom of Heaven that Christ had assured his disciples is within us all.

It had been exactly forty years since we had first heard him speak, and now we understood that his voice would be with us eternally. God had permitted us a small glimpse of His own glory that shone through the faith and love of this man. Some of us are ready to live with the fire of God burning brightly within us; others can only cope with its light and heat reflected through the presence of others. But the fire on Father Basil's lips had been bright enough to lead us along darkened paths; he had shown us the way to God by walking in light where the world cast only darkness. Now we would continue to walk supported by his prayers, through the final years until he embraced us once more.

JOURNEY TO MOUNT ATHOS

FATHER SPYRIDON BAILEY

In 2012 Father Spyridon travelled to the heart of Orthodox monasticism known as the Holy Mountain. For over a thousand years monks have dedicated their lives to the ancient pursuit of God. Journey To Mount Athos is the story of that journey and describes vividly the encounters he had with monks and hermits.
Available on Amazon and Amazon Kindle.

THE ANCIENT PATH

FATHER SPYRIDON BAILEY

In The Ancient Path Father Spyridon maintains that modern culture and philosophy has lost touch with the authentic voice of Christianity. Through a series of reflections on writings by the Fathers of the Church he identifies how it is possible to regain a true sense of reality when so much around us has entered a form of spiritual insanity.
Available on Amazon and Amazon Kindle.

TRAMPLING DOWN DEATH BY DEATH

FATHER SPYRIDON BAILEY

Only when we learn to live with a clear understanding of death and resurrection can we truly live as God intends. In Trampling Down Death By Death Father Spyridon challenges us to engage fully with our own mortality, to see beyond false and sentimental ideas about death, and embrace the full Christian understanding of what it means to live in the knowledge of our death. An inspiring and uplifting book Father Spyridon manages to treat the subject with honesty and clarity.

Available on Amazon and Amazon Kindle.

Lightning Source UK Ltd.
Milton Keynes UK
UKHW040826230322
400493UK00001B/238